# SENTRIES OF CAMELOT

## RUBY MORGAN: BOOK TWO

## L.J. RIVERS

**ISBN:** 978-82-93420-42-2

*With love,*
*for Embla, Storm, Michael and Kristiane*

# ONE

I WAS NO STRANGER TO MORNING FOG, BUT THIS WAS bordering on ridiculous. I actually had to slow down to see the Hamgate entrance to Richmond Park, and although I seldom took the time to appreciate the beauty of it, today I wouldn't have been able to. I didn't dare look at my watch for fear of running into anyone on their way to work, even if the chances were slim this early on a Saturday morning. Not that I had any chance of beating my personal best in this thick November fog anyway.

As I turned right onto the gravel path, my mind drifted to Brendan and our date for tonight—which wasn't really a date per se. We had been hanging out for a while now, not really dating—and we had yet to kiss. It wasn't that I didn't want to, but it felt like I would be misleading him. Before we could take our relationship to the next level, I had to tell him what I was—a half Fae. Every time I had tried to tell him, however, the words got stuck in my throat. There was a chance I would lose him if I did, and that would break my heart.

*Concentrate*, I said to myself, not sure if it came out aloud. But I had to focus on following the winding walkways in the park. On a sunny day, I could easily take shortcuts over lawns and through the many groves, but today I could only see a few steps ahead. My path ran parallel to Queen's Road, and although I had given up on any decent time, I pushed as fast as I dared.

I loved running at this early hour—a time Charlie had named 'half past insanity'. In the short time I had lived in London, Charlie had become the closest friend I had ever had, but unlike me, she liked to sleep in.

Today, I wasn't the only one enjoying the solitude of the morning. Behind me, the heavy steps of another jogger hit the ground at a slightly faster rhythm than mine. I slowed and carefully stepped onto the grass to let whoever it was pass by.

No one came. The footsteps had stopped.

"Hello?" The word came out a lot louder than I had planned. I swallowed, the sweat rolling down inside my compression top and windbreaker. "Hel—"

"Run, Princess!" said a voice in my left ear.

I whirled around, but there was nobody there. Only, there was—something. Someone had stood there, and all that was left was the shape of a man in the fog. And it—he—had told me to run.

Princess? The shadow had called me Princess, but I hadn't heard or seen him in over two months. I had almost started to believe I had imagined him. Was he here? Now?

"Run!" the voice repeated from the mist.

Footsteps started again from somewhere behind me. I spun back around. A black-clad man emerged from the fog. That was no jogger at all. He reached for my arm. I jerked back, jumped onto the path and dashed forward. Visibility was still virtually zero, but I had no choice. If memory served, there should be about three hundred yards to the Kingsgate exit. Usually, I could sprint that in just over thirty-five seconds, but what about the Harvester behind me?

Because it had to be a Harvester. I couldn't imagine any ordinary muggers being up this early, let alone chase joggers in the park. Besides, I knew very well how attractive my Fae blood was on the MagX market.

Surely I couldn't outrun a trained Harvester? My gut feeling gave me both the answer, "no chance in Avalon", and the alternative. I jumped out onto the grass again, sprinting towards the vague shadows of trees. If I could make it to the grove, I might have a chance zigzagging among the trunks. That could give me enough time to build a fireball or two in my hands to throw in the direction of my pursuer, and hopefully, that would be enough to scare him off.

I made it to the trees, cursing under my breath when I noticed the fog was lighter. That wasn't what I had hoped for, as this made it easier for the Harvester to follow me. I would have given my left arm to have Jen's wolf-shifting power now. Instead, I smashed my left wrist into a low hanging branch, the pain forcing a yelp out of me. I looked behind me and, sure enough, the Harvester had picked up on the sound and was heading towards me.

My blood boiled as I prepared to throw fire at him.

"That won't help you," he spat, waving his hand in front of him. The circular motion formed a shield—of magic!

He was high on MagX. Bugger!

In my right hand, a tiny ball of fire had formed. It would have to do. I threw it as hard as I could against the tree next to him. It blasted into flames, throwing bark and splinters left and right. The Harvester flinched and ducked, and I seized my chance. I swerved and ran, hoping to gain a few seconds' head start.

Sprinting out of the park through Kingsgate, I caught sight of a tiny ray of the early sun fighting its way down King's Road. The Harvester was still hot on my heels, his feet pounding the pavement, getting closer with each step. By the time I spotted the gates of White Willow University, visibility had reached safer levels. An old man was walking towards me on the pavement, twenty-odd yards ahead.

I couldn't risk his life. The Harvester might kill him if he tried to interfere, so I jumped out between a couple of parked cars and onto the street.

"Miss Morgan, is that you?" said the man. "Out for a morni—hey, you! Stop there!"

Crap! He had spotted my pursuer. This could get ugly. I had no choice but to take the Harvester on.

I was wrong.

The old man stepped into the street, holding his walking stick out. As the Harvester sprinted past him, the man swung his cane, sweeping the Harvester off his feet. My pursuer fell flat on his face. He tried to get up, but the old man hit him hard on his lower back with the cane. The Harvester squirmed in pain.

"Get away from her," the old man hissed. "Or suffer the consequences."

I started towards them, ready to throw a force field around the man if the Harvester tried to fight him. To my relief, the bastard seemed to realise he had lost his edge. He rolled sideways, got to his feet and sprinted down the street. It seemed a bit odd that he would run from an old man, but the effects of the MagX must have started to fade.

For a second, it looked like the old man considered following him, but he stayed put. He turned to me instead. The first time I had seen the professor, he had worn something out of the colonial 1800s. Now, he was dressed in yet another old-fashioned outfit, tailored and perfectly fitted, but this looked more like what I imagined Victorian fashion looked like. A blue dress coat ended right below his knees, and I could just make out the white vest underneath the broad lapels. His lavender trousers matched the gloves that folded around the head of his cane.

I hadn't seen him since he helped Charlie and me find the old blueprints of the uni campus, which made it possible to locate Jen in the discontinued boiler room. I almost lost the other of my newfound friends that night. I had only known Jen for a short while, but she had become almost as close a friend as Charlie was.

Charlie was human, but I trusted her completely with my secret, and Jen was a Mag herself. A Shifter, who could turn into the most magnificent white wolf. After Charlie and I saved Jen from the crazy Harvesters, who had already killed two girls and were trying to drain Jen's blood, we had become closer than I had ever been with anyone, other than my mum and dad.

"Professor Kaine," I called and approached him. "Are you ok?"

He looked genuinely surprised at my question. "Why, yes. Of course I am. But more importantly, are you, Miss Morgan?"

I glanced down the street as the Harvester turned left onto Crescent Road. I suspected it wasn't the last I would see of him.

"How did you—?"

"Are you unharmed, child?"

"Yes, Professor. I bumped my arm, but nothing serious. We should—"

"You should go home and have a warm shower and some breakfast. I think I will change my planned route for this morning's walk. I very much dislike change, but today I believe it is justified."

I smiled. "I believe you are right, sir. Thank you so much for—" I pointed down the street. "For your help."

He scoffed. "Damned purse-snatcher. I should have given him a thorough pummelling, made sure he remembered me."

Not commenting on the purse snatching, I let out a little laugh. "I don't think he'll forget you, Professor. That handle seems quite heavy."

He lifted the cane, showing me the large white handle. It looked expensive, and not at all Victorian in style. A snake curled itself along the top inches of the dark brown wood, turning into a big knot at the top.

"The cane itself is ebony," Kaine said. "The handle is somewhat illegal, I'm afraid. At least in this day and age. Ivory, hand-carved in Kenya, more than two centuries ago."

"That's really old. An heirloom?"

"Something like that. Well, I'll be on my way, young lady. And you had better get that arm looked at, just in case."

"I will. Thank you again, Professor."

"Nonsense," he puffed, smiling.

I watched him stroll across the street, his old legs floating like he was a dancer in a 1940s musical film—the morning light filtering through the remains of the fog actually made him appear in black and white. I turned and headed through the campus gates.

The pain in my left wrist was getting more intense. It had started to swell and had adopted at least three different shades of blue. I moved my fingers, slowly at first, then made a fist. It hurt, but not too much. As I was also able to move the wrist itself, I concluded that nothing was broken.

The swelling threatened to crack the lock on my pulse watch, however, so I removed it. The screen told me it was still only 7.32, and although I had stopped running many minutes ago, my heart rate was touching on ninety per cent.

I looked around. Nobody else was out. I had to try,

even though I knew very well that we Fae could only heal others, not ourselves.

I placed my right hand over the predominantly purple swelling and closed my eyes. The surge of magic in my veins and nerves was an intoxicating experience —one I had always loved and never tired of. The tiny hairs rose on the back of my neck. I sent a flow of magic healing through my hand and into the injured wrist, feeling the heat move through the muscles and sinew. Beads of sweat sizzled on my skin, but I knew it wouldn't burn me. After all, only weeks ago, I held fireballs in my hands without getting a single mark.

I noticed I'd been holding my breath. Releasing the grip, I also let the air out of my lungs, letting go of the magic rush. The pain in my wrist was very much still there.

*Oh well. I had to try, didn't I?*

I was soaked and needed a shower. Back at the flat, however, Charlie and Jen would be fast asleep, and I didn't want to risk waking them. And since my stomach was growling, I walked towards Brady's instead. A hot cup of green tea and one of their freshly baked scones might help calm me down.

"Shit, that looks terrible," Nick said.

I hadn't noticed him when I walked in. All I could think of was the tea and scone on the table in front of me.

"Trust me, this is nothing. What are you doing here so early?" I asked.

He nodded at the table on the far side, stacks of books almost hiding his laptop.

"I have a shitload of reading to do, and our flat smells just as bad as it looks. I had planned to watch West Ham beat the crap out of Tottenham later, a task they will fail miserably at, of course. But Jack and Reece came over last night, and we all sort of drowned ourselves, and well—never mind that. What happened to your arm?"

"I slipped on some wet leaves and twisted it on the landing, I guess. It's just a sprain."

"Sure? Looks like it might be broken. You should have it looked at."

Before I could tell him about my expert medical examination and conclusion, the door sprung open. My favourite wolf rushed in, although in her equally beautiful human form.

"What do you mean, broken?" she said as she came running towards our table. "Are you hurt, Ru?"

"How did you hear that?" Nick said.

Jen still hadn't warmed to him after his anti-Mag rant at the pub one night during Freshers' Week. She shrugged. "You were loud."

I bit my lip to quell the laughter, and had to focus on Jen's eyes to avoid looking at Nick. I knew very well about her hearing, which had to be five times better than a human's, if not more.

"I didn't break anything," I said. "It's just a sprained wrist, chillax."

Jen turned to Nick. "And what are you doing here?"

"Hey, when are you going to give me a break? I've said I'm sorry a dozen times already."

"I don't think you mean it, is all."

"Whatever." Nick waved her off. "Get that arm looked at, Ruby, ok? I'll leave you girls to it, and return to the separation of power and reform in post-cold war Russia."

"See you at work," I said and turned to Jen again. "He's actually quite nice," I whispered as he walked away.

"Yeah, yeah—a nice racist. Like that Colbert guy."

"Colbert? Ah, you mean Colburn," I said. "He's creepy. But no, Nick's not like that at all."

And that was the truth. Jarl Colburn was the quintessential creep if I ever saw one. He claimed to be a family man, a devoted Christian who loved everyone.

*Yeah, right.*

The last time I saw him was in a clip from one of his sermons. Church of Purity, he called his congregation. What had he called the Magicals again? 'Spawn of Satan, children of the fallen angels.'

In Colburn's eyes, Magicals should be incarcerated and kept away from humans. His booming voice still resonated in my head: To keep God's Earth pure, as He intended when He created us in His image.

"Earth to Ruby?"

"Huh?"

"Seems I lost you there, babe," said Jen. "Get back to your broken arm, will you? What happened?"

It was my turn to wave her off. "It's really just a sprain, not even that. Where have you been this early? I thought you'd be fast asleep." I looked at her clothes, every bit as wet as mine, though grimier, as if they had been stomped into the dirt before she put them on. "You've been roaming again?"

She winked. "Caught me a little breakfast, yes. Want the details?"

I held my hand up to stop her. "No, please! If I never hear about your devouring of small animals again, it'll still be too soon."

She laughed. "Don't worry, I have no desire to have your vomit all over my shoes again."

I leaned forward. "But something happened this morning."

Even though she could have heard my whisper two football fields away, Jen also leaned forward. I told her about the Harvester, and how Professor Kaine helped me.

"Saved me, I should say."

She narrowed her eyes. "I think he saved the Harvester, no?"

Sometimes, I hadn't quite figured out when, her perfect English was supplemented with the tiniest hint of an accent. Her French heritage could be heard in the very occasional in words like "think", or—like now— that little "no" at the end.

"You're probably right," I replied. "I'm glad I didn't have to use magic in front of Kaine. But I would have, of course, if it came to that."

"I only wish I had taken a different route," she said between her teeth.

I nodded, having thought the same. With Jen by my side in her wolf form, the Harvester would've had no chance whatsoever.

"Let's go home," Jen said. "I desperately need a shower, and so do you. And get some ice on that wrist."

"I tried to heal it," I said. "Didn't work."

"Good."

"What do you mean, good?"

"We don't need you having even more magic powers, ok? You're already a Fae goddess with to-die-for locks of hair. Leave some of the spotlight to the rest of us, will you?" She gave me a nudge.

"Half Fae." I laughed.

# TWO

I STARED AT BRENDAN IN THE DARKNESS OF THE CINEMA. The last glare from the credits flickered on the screen, casting streaks of shadows and light on his skin, enhancing the features of his face—his chiselled jawline, the slight stubble on his defined cheeks, and the one dimple, which appeared when he caught me looking. His hand went over the armrest, his fingers tracing my arm and my almost healed wrist, finally finding my hand and knitting his carefully in mine.

I smiled and turned back to pretend to look at the credits. A girl named Wendy Cho was 'Best boy grip'. I bet she got a few 'who's a good boy' comments when she told her friends about it.

"I think we can leave now," Brendan whispered in my ear.

I nodded. My shift was over, this was the last screening of the night, and we were the only ones left apart from Nick, who had promised to finish the last sweep of popcorn and clean the stands. All I had to do was turn off the lights and lock up. The job itself was nothing short of boring, but it had its perks, with free films and getting to hang out with Brendan while being paid at the same time. Or simply a quiet couple of hours to catch up on my studies or write something for the Whisper.

Nick had started growing on me, as well. The first encounter I had with him had not placed him in my corner. He had been loud, drunk and trashing Mags to his friends at the Old Willow pub. Like Brendan, he didn't know that I was one of the Mags he had said 'were not people'.

We stood, easing out between the seat rows and back up the stairs into the empty foyer. Nick had apparently left already. Most of the lights were off, and he had done a surprisingly good job cleaning. He had even emptied all the bins before he left. In the ticket booth, his playing cards lay spread out on the table—most likely a half-finished solitaire game left for tomorrow. "I like how real the cards feel in my hands," he had said when I asked why he didn't play on his laptop instead.

Sober Nick was much nicer than drunken Nick. Besides, he wasn't alone in his thoughts about Mags. Being half Fae, I had learned to deal with that kind of prejudice regularly.

Brendan turned off the last light switch with one hand, giving me a gentle squeeze with the other. I smiled at him, well aware that he had similar thoughts to Nick's where Mags were concerned. He wasn't loud about it, but seeing as his sister ran off with a Mag who had played mind tricks on their parents and conned them into cleaning out their bank accounts, I could understand where he was coming from. I just wished one Mag didn't speak for all of us.

I didn't like that word—Mag—but it was the one society had taken to, as an umbrella term for all Magicals, no matter the level of purity in our blood. There were other names used for those like me, and Mag was hardly the worst of the bunch. On the tube, one would invariably pass graffiti with 'Go home, Maggers'. I seriously doubted any of the spray painters knew about Avalon, so what they meant by 'home' was beyond me. Only a week before our film night, I overheard a student who mentioned "those Maggots" when the BBC news anchor on one of Brady's TV screens used what had become the more politically correct term: 'the M-word'.

I turned the key and punched in the code for the alarm before we started towards the bus stop. There were lots of people all around us, dressed up for a Saturday night out. I zipped up my jacket and buried my chin underneath the collar. The air sent chills across my skin, but it didn't seem to bother any of the girls wearing miniskirts and tank tops.

"You can have my jacket if you want," Brendan said, eyeing me gently.

"I'm all right," I replied and snuggled closer to him. "Especially if you hold me." I never had to ask him twice, and though we had yet to put a label on our relationship, there was an undeniable spark between us.

We sat on the bench at the bus stop, the warmth from his body making the cold stay off my skin.

Somehow I had to tell him about me, but the fear of losing him still kept the words from coming out. I already had one bad experience of keeping the truth from my first real boyfriend, Zack, and I never wanted to relive that moment of someone looking at me like he had. A look of ice-cold fear.

Zack never told anyone about me, perhaps because I told him I would turn him into a toad if he did. He seemed to believe that not only was I capable of such a thing, but that I would actually do it. Instead, he spread nasty rumours about how I was supposedly a slut and had cheated on him, and for a whole year, I had to eat lunch at Blacon High School by myself, walk home alone, and was ignored by my classmates. A high price to pay to keep my secret, but one I accepted, if not gladly. That was before I immersed myself with work at the local newspaper as an intern journalist, catching the eye of my creepy editor, Logan.

I sighed at the memories, wriggling out of Brendan's embrace.

He frowned at me. "Are we good?"

"I'm just warm enough now," I lied.

His next words were muffled by the shriek of sirens. Three police cars whooshed by at full speed, and an ambulance passed moments later before the bus finally arrived, and we stepped inside. I put my Oyster card down on the registration panel, and we found a couple of seats in front on the second level. As the bus drove off, I watched the beams of blue lights pan across the river while the sirens faded away.

Brendan leaned forward, clearly watching the same thing I was. "There's been a lot of sirens lately."

"This is London," I murmured, while the Harvester from this morning weighed on my mind.

"I know, but it feels like a lot more than usual. Crime rates are up in this part of London, too."

I tilted my head at him.

He shrugged. "I checked. As a future detective, I need to stay alert."

"So, how high are we talking?"

He breathed deeply, then leaned back in his seat. "Very. And not only that, but there's been an increase in the number of casualties, too. People seem to be attacking the coppers, and they respond to the violence with bullets. I don't know what has got everyone so riled up, though I have my suspicions."

I was afraid to ask as I had suspicions of my own, but I couldn't help myself. "Which are?"

"MagX. There's a lot of it on the market now, and when people take it, thinking they become invincible, they go on a complete bender, no longer in control at all."

What he said made sense. MagX was a dangerous drug for humans to take, more so than any other drug on the market. Charlie had once said it made people feel like superheroes. That might very well be true, but not long after she said that I'd had to save her from an overdose of a bad strip of blood. She would have died from a heart attack if I didn't have my healing power. Possible loss of life was a bad trade for a few hours of superpowers.

"I've never known people to become especially aggressive on MagX, though," I blurted, allowing my thoughts to spill out. Me and my mouth. This wasn't the kind of topic I had wanted us to discuss, yet here I was, encouraging him.

"It's not been a big issue, no, but who knows? If there's a bad batch of blood somewhere, the effects could very well cause violence. I think the dealers dilute the stuff to make more money, and then it gets tainted and really dangerous."

To my relief, the bus screen showed White Willow University as the next stop, and we found our way down to the first level. I stumbled as the bus hurried over a speed bump, falling into Brendan's arms.

"Well, well, Milady Morgan." He gave me a smouldering look, taking my hand, then arched my back over his arm. He bent down, gazing deeply into my eyes. He was so close. His breath smelled of butter and caramel popcorn as his lips parted. A few strands of his chestnut-coloured hair tickled my forehead. I lifted my chin, and he closed his eyes.

The bus screeched to a stop, and we both toppled over. Entangled on the bus floor, we burst out laughing.

"Getting off?" the bus driver called, an annoyed tone in her voice.

"Yep," replied Brendan.

"Get off then."

We scrambled to our feet, rushed outside and entered the gates to campus. The air was misty, a thin sheet of fog forming over the large lake. It was going to rain again soon.

"I've had fun, Ruby." Brendan cleared his throat. "I was kind of hoping the evening wouldn't end just yet."

Crap! What was I going to say? I didn't want it to end either, but I knew all too well what would happen if I went back to his place after the evening we'd just had. And I could not live with myself if I hurt him.

"That would be great," I said. "But I'm already way behind on a story for The Whispering Willow. Rae will kill me if I don't have it ready by the morning. Then there's the task for my Source Criticism class I need to finish."

He put his hands in his jeans pockets, and never mentioned that tomorrow was Sunday as he swayed a little on his feet before motioning towards Craydon House.

"Least I can do is walk the lady home then."

"I'd like that."

Brendan followed me all the way to the front door, where we said our goodbyes. I had killed the mood already, so he didn't attempt another kiss. I wanted him to, though. By the powers of magic, I wanted it so bad. But I couldn't. I had to find some way to tell him what I was without scaring him off. But how?

Tiptoeing down the hallway, I had almost reached the door to my room when someone coughed behind me.

"Honestly, Ru. You think you can get away from me grilling you about your date?" Charlie said, tapping her foot. Her small frame did not detract from her authoritative nature.

"Someone say date?" Jen stuck her head out of her

room, then stepped into the hallway to stand more than a head taller than Charlie.

I threw my hands up in mock surrender. There was no way they would let me off the hook. "Very well. My room, if you want me to tell."

They nodded and joined me. I feigned annoyance, but it didn't last long. These were my friends, and it was unbelievably good to have them on my side. Though I didn't think I had much to tell, they listened.

"And that's pretty much it," I said, ending my recount of the night.

"Oh, dude! Still no kiss?" Charlie pouted.

"Good." Jen sat on the windowsill, painting her toenails. "Make him work for it, woman. Who says we have to give anything before we decide we're ready? Kissing is an intimate affair. We shouldn't hand ourselves out to every man who looks our way."

Charlie gave Jen a sideways glance, and Jen smirked.

"It doesn't mean we can't give ourselves to every man who looks our way either." She winked at me. "It's called freedom of choice."

Charlie smiled then, and we laughed and chatted for a while longer before I turned my laptop on.

"Now, I actually do have a story to write for The Whisper. Granted, the deadline is tomorrow evening, but I'd like to get a head start."

We said goodnight, and I turned to the screen. Instead of opening Word to write my story, I browsed the news headlines going back a few months. Brendan was right. There was definitely an unusual spike of violence against police officers. Did my pursuer from the park have anything to do with this? If so, why? The stories were vague at best. DCI Davies was about the only one making statements. I remembered him well from the time when Jen was kidnapped. He had been friendly toward me. The same could not be said about his colleague, PC Paddock.

I had worried a lot for the first weeks after those horrid events, about whether the blood-harvesting janitor would blow the whistle on me and tell the police what I had done. He had seen me essentially become a magical bomb.

And then he had killed himself in his cell. It made headlines across all the national newspapers. *The Willow murderer commits suicide.* Some said the world was better off, though quite a few people seemed to be sorry he was gone. There had been a massive amount of roses and candles placed outside the prison in his memory. Me? I was glad he was dead. He could never hurt anyone ever again. I was firmly against the death penalty, but as he did this to himself, I would not shed a tear for that monster.

My eyes drooped. I would have to finish my article the next day, after all.

As I slid under the covers, my phone lit up. Squinting, I brought the phone under the duvet and ducked down to read the message.

*I know you're busy tomorrow. But may I court you again on Monday?*

I tapped my finger on the screen to reply.

*You may try, milord.*

Moments later, he answered again.

*Then I shall call it a date if that's all right by you.*
*Say eight? I'll meet you by the gates.*

My stomach somersaulted.

*It's a date!*
*Sleep well, milady.*
*You too, milord.*

Smiling, I closed my eyes and slept.

# THREE

I WAS DRIPPING WET—AGAIN—BOTH FROM THE SWEAT ON my skin and the light drizzle of rain after my run. I had stayed on campus this morning, running laps around the lake. Yesterday was the first time I had strayed from my routine. I did have a lot to work on, and there was always plenty of time to run, so I ended up convincing myself to do the whole lazy Sunday routine instead. Sweatpants, t-shirt, legs on the table, laptop, and about half a dozen cups of green tea. All part of a subconscious—or rather deliberate, if I was being honest with myself—plan to stay away from the park. In fact, there was no way I would return to Richmond Park for my runs any time soon. At least not in this kind of weather. I had to find another route, though. If not for anything else than for sheer motivation, as the laps around the campus lake were beginning to feel tedious already.

I glanced at the water, half expecting to see a shadowy figure somewhere, but everything seemed normal. Between school and work, I had hardly thought about the shadow at all for the past few weeks —not until it spoke to me on Saturday. It had to be the shadow, warning me about the Harvester.

And I had yet to see Mum, so we hadn't even had a chance to talk about it. It was not an issue for a phone call, it had to be face to face. She had promised to tell me what it was and warned me to stay away. But it didn't feel dangerous. Rather it felt like, whatever it was, it wanted to protect me. Mum would just have to tell me what she knew when I went home for Christmas. If I could wait that long. I didn't like being kept in the dark.

I ran past the white willow and back to Craydon to get ready for class, and an hour later, I had found a seat in the lecture hall. Showered and clean, ready to soak up all the knowledge I could.

"Confirm your sources. Check and check again. We are not fiction writers, we are truth seekers, and your job will be to tell the world about the things that move in the shadows." Mr Zhang, my lecturer on journalistic criticism, clearly had a thousand ways to explain the exact same topic, and the takeaway was always the same: be critical, check your sources, find the truth, and whatever you do, tell the real story because the people deserve to know. He had been playing the same tune since the first lecture I attended with him in September, and though it was repetitive, I appreciated his firm persuasion for the truth.

"How can you tell?" Frank, Mr Zhang's self-appointed technical assistant, had his hand up but spoke before he was given the word.

"You can't." Mr Zhang dipped his head at Frank. "And I would appreciate it if you did not speak out of turn again. If I was back teaching in China, this would be completely unacceptable, Mr Hanson. Rudeness aside, your question has merit. How can we tell truth from lies?"

A few hands shot up throughout the room. I rarely raised my hand in Mr Zhang's class, however. He would always prod for more than I was willing to give, and sometimes more than I knew how to answer at all.

"Miss Morgan," Mr Zhang said. "Any thoughts?"

*Crap! Really?* "I guess—" I turned my ring around my finger, contemplating what to say. "I guess, as you said, you can't ever know for sure. What you can do is gather as much information as possible, check it against each other, and see if the pattern fits."

He gave me a stiff smile, the kind that never reached his eyes. "A fair assessment. How do you say? If it walks like a kitten and runs like a cat?"

Vicky, who sat next to me, snorted, then called out, "If it looks like a duck, and quacks like a duck, then it probably is a duck."

"Precisely. Very good, Miss Jenkins."

Although I wanted to say something about how Jenkins forgot about "if it swims like a duck", my mind was on the subject of discussion. My hand rose, and Mr Zhang tilted his head at me to speak.

"While I agree that people should know the truth, what about the truth that can hurt people, should we also tell those kinds of truths?" My mouth was blabbing away again. "And how about the ethical aspect of it all?

It's not like everyone wants their secrets told to the world, it might even be dangerous to expose certain things. I mean, don't we have a responsibility to protect and serve—I know, wrong profession, but still?"

The lecturer smiled at me then, a genuine kind of smile I had not seen from him before. "Well, Miss Morgan. Those are excellent questions. Sounds to me like you're on the right trail."

"Track," Vicky muttered into her coffee can.

Mr Zhang ignored her and stepped behind his desk. "In fact, I want you all to do a task on these exact questions. Find three main predicaments you might come across as a journalist, then reflect on these issues and make ethical and professional arguments on how to handle them. The task will be on the course page under assignments, and I expect you to deliver it on time as per the deadline stated. That will be all for today."

The sound of laptops closing, zippers being pulled and chairs screeching, was followed by chattering students as they left the lecture room. I sat for a moment, staring at the ruby on my ring. It had been seven years since my dad died of a MagX overdose, and I had looked for the truth in every dusty dark corner I could find. So far, I had come up empty-handed. It bothered me that I had not been able to figure it out. I knew he had MagX in his system when he was found, and the doctors had been clear about his diagnosis: a drug-induced heart attack. The thing that bothered me was the fact that it wasn't like him at all. He hated the entire MagX industry almost as much as I did.

"You all right there, Miss Morgan?" Mr Zhang leaned over me—or rather, more like leaned in, as he was not much taller standing than I was sitting down.

"I was just thinking about the truth," I said.

"What would it change?"

"Not sure."

Would it change anything if I knew where Dad had got the drug or how it ended up killing him? Why did it matter so much? He was dead either way, and I missed him so much.

"You had some pertinent questions before," said Mr Zhang. "Sometimes we're better off not knowing. There are times when not knowing makes us happier. Still, most of the time, the truth will set you free." He chuckled to himself. "I got that one right, I believe?"

I nodded. "Thank you. I've got to run now, but I'll see you next week." I dropped my laptop into my bag and made my way out of the lecture hall.

My bag vibrated, and I fished my phone out. There was no caller ID, and I didn't recognize the number. I pursed my lips, then swiped open the message.

Need to talk. Ring me as soon as you have a few. P.

P? I shook my head at the phone as I walked down the cobbled pathway from the lecture hall, leading to the far side of Craydon Court. Logan Whelk, my old editor back in Cheshire, when I was interning at Blacon Press, had taught me many things. And aside from the fact that he was a total scumbag, and that I really should put a MeToo hashtag next to his face and post it online, he had a fair bit of journalistic insight. One thing he taught me that I agreed on, was to never allow a good story to pass me by. I plugged my earphones in and returned the call.

"Paddock," the voice on the other end said.

I gaped. Why was he contacting me? It was weeks since the case of the Willow Murderer had been closed. PC Paddock was one of the police officers who had investigated the missing girls, and I hadn't seen him since the day they caught the janitor. The officer hadn't been my favourite person, and I couldn't imagine I was his either. The looks he had given me during the investigation made my skin crawl. On top of that, he seemed less than taken with the prospects of Mags in his precinct. What did he want from me now?

"This is Ruby Morgan. You need to talk?"

"Miss Morgan. Yes. I'm happy you returned my call." His voice was as I remembered it: stern, with a cold edge, his cockney accent apparent in 'appy' and 'me call'.

But something in his voice sounded different, almost like he was scared. "I can't talk on the phone, but we need to meet. When are you free?"

I hesitated. Paddock was the last person I wanted to see, with the obvious exception of the Harvester from Richmond Park, but it sounded like it might be important.

"I'm free tonight," I told him.

"Perfect. I can meet you in Richmond Park at nine. Walk into the main entrance, and I'll make sure you find me." He hung up.

Alarm bells went off like crazy in my head at the mention of the park. For a second I wanted to call him back and say no, perhaps have him meet me someplace else. But he had sounded desperate, and that triggered my curiosity.

Besides, there was another issue that bothered me more than going back to Richmond Park.

There goes my date with Brendan, I thought. He had promised to court me again today, although I had yet to hear a word from him since we agreed on making it a date. I sent him a quick text to tell him I got caught up in some girl stuff. The fact that I was lying to him—again—was not lost on me. As I neared the white willow, he texted back.

I'll court you another day. Got some stuff of my own to sort out.

I narrowed my eyes at the text. No emoji? Not even an x at the end? Maybe he was insulted that I cancelled on him, or more likely he was simply busy, and it shouldn't bother me.

But it did.

Charlie and Jen were already waiting for me underneath the willow. Jen had her feet in the water, and Charlie was on her back, reading a book. Fiction, by the looks of it. Seemed she was taking a study break.

"Red!" Jen called.

I sped up, then dumped down between them on the large blanket they had folded out. The grass was still a little damp after the heavy rainfall, but the fog had cleared. Students scurried back and forth beside the lake and between buildings, and a couple of squirrels chased each other around the trunk of the willow. The drizzle from this morning had ceased, and it was now a lovely day. And yet my nerves were on edge. My gaze flitted around the lake, my body alert in case someone decided to jump out and attack me.

Get a grip, Ru! Not even a Harvester would attack me in the middle of campus in broad daylight. I was almost certain that was right.

"You clean up good," I said to Jen, shaking off the feeling of being watched.

"I do."

Charlie closed the book and sat next to me. "Herself, sure. Her bathroom, not so much. And the laundry room stinks." She waved her arms at Jen. "Where on earth did you leave your clothes?"

Jen shrugged. "I forgot to bring a bag for them the other day, and they got caught in the rain. Then I forgot about them until this morning. It happens."

Charlie shook her head and picked up her vibrating phone from the blanket. "Duncan! I have to take this. See you at home." She grabbed her book and her bag, then started off walking and talking.

It had been a couple of weeks since we all saw Duncan last. Ilyana's murder had hit him hard, and he had locked himself in his room for the first week before he announced he was going on the straight and narrow to get rid of his MagX addiction. Now, he was in rehab. I hoped he would pull through and never touch the stuff again.

"What's up?" Jen asked as she fell on her back and air-dried her feet. "Still thinking about that Harvester?"

"Actually, not so much. I got a text from PC Paddock, and then I spoke to him."

"Paddock? The copper working Ilyana's case?"

"That's the one." I looked around and watched the small figure that was Charlie skip up the steps to Craydon Court. Lowering my voice, I continued, "He wants me to meet him tonight, in Richmond Park."

Jen's lip curled up into the beginning of a sneer. "You're not going alone."

"Kind of hoped you would say that." I smiled at her then glanced back as Charlie disappeared inside our house. "Do we tell Charlie?"

"That girl is as fierce as they come, but she's human. If Paddock is dealing in some shady stuff, then we don't want her in the middle of it."

"I'm not sure. I feel bad leaving her out of the loop, but I have no idea what Paddock wants from me."

The sneer on Jen's face was replaced by a smirk. "Mon chéri, what could any man want from you? That wild red hair is doing you no favours, and your wardrobe could use a serious do-over, but babe, you're gorgeous."

I stuck my tongue out. "I'm pretty sure he doesn't want that."

"Even so, I've got your back."

I did feel better with Jen by my side. I had seen her wolf. She was caught off guard when she was kidnapped—by her date, no less—and I was certain she would never allow anyone to get that close to hurting her ever again. It was good that she stayed on her toes, and that I could count on her, but I hoped she wouldn't close herself down completely from creating new relationships either. She had turned down at least five boys I knew of already since the incident.

"If we're going on a mission tonight, we'll need to dress the part." Jen slid her feet into a pair of sandals, which were not at all season-appropriate, before we rolled up the blanket and started home.

I shook my head. "It'll be dark, and we're meeting with Paddock. I'll wear what I'm wearing now."

She shrugged. "We'll see about that."

We were trotting back towards Craydon when a boy skated past us. I stopped mid-step, which my Converses were not designed to cope with, especially on the slippery leaves, and tried desperately to find my balance. As a second skater flew past, I jumped back to avoid him, my foot slipping, this time sending me flat on my back. I found myself in what I guessed would have made an excellent fail clip on YouTube. Luckily, I didn't hit my head upon landing, but I was certainly going to have a hard time sitting in classes tomorrow—my bum taking the bulk of the impact.

I tried pushing myself upright when a jolt of light hit my eyes so hard it felt like it was pushing me to stay down. The campus slowly disappeared before me, all the buildings, the iron gates and the big white willow, which had given the university its name, were also gone. Instead, a scene played out in front of my eyes, as if it was part of the film I watched with Brendan on Saturday. This was no romantic comedy, though.

Three kids in hoodies and caps were crouching behind a concrete block full of graffiti tags. One of the boys was shouting something, but I couldn't hear the words over the—what was that, an explosion? The concrete block was slanted to one side, and next to it lay a skateboard upside down, its wheels slowly turning to a halt. A bowl to the right and a halfpipe—or maybe a quarter, I never learned the difference—completed the skatepark scene.

A police officer grabbed one of the kids, a girl, and something like a force field erupted in the space between them, propelling the officer away from her. Another explosion—no, a gunshot—echoed in my mind.

A gush of blood sprayed over the grey concrete as the girl's body slumped. Her head hit the ground with a sickening thud, her face frozen in a terrified grimace.

Blue sparks lit up, and one of the boys dropped to his back, spasming wildly as the sparks kept flying. I tried to stand, but my feet wouldn't obey. I wanted to help the kids—heal them.

In a split second, the skatepark vanished, and I was back on the ground by Craydon. What in the name of Lady Nimue was that? It was so incredibly real!

"Need a hand?" Jen stretched her arm out and pulled me to my feet. "For a medallist runner, you're a real klutz sometimes."

I brushed down my clothes, and Jen helped remove the leaves sticking to my back. "That," I said, "has never happened before."

"You mean you've never taken a swan dive like that?" She raised her brows. "Sure!"

"No, I mean, I saw ... something."

We sat on the bench below our flat. Jen crossed her

legs, then looked at me without a word, providing me time to gather my thoughts.

"I think I ... might have a new power."

"You're effing kidding me!" Jen shook her head. "Sorry. Go on."

"When I fell, I saw something. Like, maybe, a vision of sorts? I don't know. There were these kids at a skatepark, there were police there, and a girl died in front of me."

I knitted my hands together, my finger tracing the ruby on my ring, feeling the chip that was not visible to the naked eye. What else could it be other than a vision? It was so vivid, and I had even smelled the gunpowder, hadn't I? Receiving my firepower had been one too many powers than I thought I would get, but this? This was some high-level magic. Mum had always told me it was a rare gift to see the future—if that was what I had seen—a gift not even she had. And Mum was a Pure.

"Honestly, Ru, you're beginning to freak me out." Jen straightened her ponytail.

"Why?"

"I told you not to amp up your magic, yet here you are, doing just that." She cleaned her teeth with one of her manicured nails, then softened her tone. "If this is a new power, then this is serious. A girl is dead, or about to be."

"Not if I can help it."

It did feel like it was indeed very serious. And the face of the dead girl had already begun haunting my mind. I could feel the image of her pushing to the forefront. But had it already happened, or was it, as Jen said, about to happen?

Shaking my head free of the repeating vision, I took Jen's hand. "There were policemen there. Makes me think this has something to do with Paddock."

"Then we really don't want Charlie involved."

I nodded. There was no way I was going to risk Charlie's life.

# FOUR

I TIPTOED DOWN THE HALLWAY AS GWEN STEFANI BELTED out "Baby Don't Lie" from Charlie's room. It would likely be enough to muffle my steps, but Charlie had a sixth sense about these things, so I decided to play it safe. The main door opened with a familiar squeak that made me freeze to look back down the hall. Charlie's door was still closed.

I exhaled slowly and slipped outside.

The cool wind swept over campus, sending leaves flying off in the air. The skies had cleared, but it was cold enough to make me happy I'd brought a scarf, although it totally clashed with the outfit Jen had left for me. I looked like a glammed-up version of Lara Croft in the tight-fitting leather trousers, which were definitely not something you would find at Primark. The top I was wearing had a neckline that made me uncomfortable, even with the ends of my blue scarf—which was from Primark—tucked into it.

Jen was already by the campus gates when I walked

up to her. She had said she was going out with her study group earlier, though I was fairly certain she wasn't in one at the moment and had said that for Charlie's benefit.

"There you are," she said, tilting her head to look at me. "Count on you to mess up a stunning outfit. At least, wear it like you mean it." She pulled the scarf up from my neckline and batted it in the air, then wrapped it carefully back around in gentle hoops.

"It's cold," I said.

"You'd think someone with firepower could handle a slightly chilly November evening."

I laughed, and we started down the road towards Richmond Park. "We can't all be furballs like you."

"True. To be fair, it needs to be Antarctica cold before my teeth chatter."

Long shadows stretched across the road, and I turned my head back and forth several times over, not able to hide my nerves one bit.

Jen caught my gaze. "Worried about that stalker from the other day?"

"Aren't you?"

She shrugged. "My nose won't betray me again. No one will catch me with my guard down after what happened last time."

I took her arm. "I'm glad you're here."

"And I you. Even if your fashion style is seriously damaged."

I gave her a friendly slap and almost forgot about being scared of what might hide in the dark. If Jen said her nose would protect us, I believed her. We continued to walk briskly forwards while playing our new favourite game, Breaking Mag, in which we tried to guess which celebrities were Mags and what powers they had. There weren't really any winners because none of us knew the real truth, but it was fun to pretend.

There were a lot more of us in the world than people knew about, although some bloodlines had become washed out to the point where someone with Mags in their lineage wasn't guaranteed to gain any powers at all. According to Mum, my grandad was convinced that the whole Magical community had been weakened by mixing with humans, and it was hard to disagree. I should know, being the product of a mixed marriage myself.

The main difference between my estranged grandad's view and mine was that I preferred to look at it as evolution. Mags and humans shared everything but the magic, and maybe that was more important in the long run. Evolution brings us closer, which I happened to think was good, as opposed to the views of Jarl Colburn and his followers.

As I was contemplating Jen's latest suggestion, Lady Gaga, whom she meant was too good to be one hundred per cent human, she halted in front of the entrance to the park. Her arm was wrapped around mine so tightly that I was forced to stop too.

"Ready?" she said.

"Not at all," I admitted as I took in the darkness beyond the fence. "So, let's go inside."

Jen nodded, and we stepped into the park. How on

earth were we supposed to find Paddock in here? There were a few lights on the path, but otherwise, the rest was firmly in the shadows.

Something flashed between the trees to my right. It disappeared, then flashed again. It seemed deliberate, almost like a signal.

"Morse code," Jen said. "That's him."

"What? How do you know?"

"I know Morse code."

I raised my eyebrows at her. Most people wouldn't have been able to tell in the dark, but her wolf sight would get the message clearly enough.

She snickered. "Of course I don't know Morse code. I smell him, is all."

That, on the other hand, I believed.

We made our way across the grass, shuffling through the leaves. The wind was more gracious between the large oaks in the park, taking the edge off the cold underneath the canopies.

"Ruby Morgan?" a voice whispered.

"I'm here."

"Good." Paddock moved out from behind a trunk, flashlight in hand, though the light was off. "Come."

We followed him into a thicket of trees and bushes, and I hoped I wasn't about to ruin Jen's expensive clothes on all the branches clawing at me. The leather turned out to be quite efficient, however, as the branches never pierced the clothes or got stuck in them. Anything from my own wardrobe would have been fit to throw out after this walk.

Paddock stopped abruptly, then turned back to us.

He turned the flashlight on, and though he pointed it downwards, it lit up the features of his face and made him look like something out of my worst nightmares. His jawline was sheathed in darkness, his cheekbones white against the light. He wore a cap, but the beam from the flashlight made his eyes look gaunt.

"Why is she here?" he hissed, staring at Jen.

"Backup." Jen crossed her arms.

Great start, I thought, sighing audibly. "You can trust her." The question was, could we trust him?

"I hope you're right. I guess, after everything, it might be good that she's come."

Whatever game he was playing at, I sure as eggs wasn't going to play this one. "Cut to the chase, all right. I'm cold, and this park gives me the heebie-jeebies."

His face softened weirdly as he moved his hand and the light flickered across his face. "I apologise for the inconvenience, ladies. This is the best blind spot I could find. No one can know that I'm here. There are cameras everywhere, and I don't know how many bugs and wires there might be at my house, or anywhere else I usually go."

All right, he had my attention. "Well, go on then," I said, my voice lowered.

"I think we better start with this." He dug out something from one of the many pockets in what looked like trousers designed for hiking, then handed me a picture.

Jen bumped my shoulder. "That's you!"

It was me. At a quick glance, the picture itself was nothing special, though looking closely, it was one that I thought was destroyed. It showed me, standing in my running gear by the lake. A misty fog spread out above the water, and I remembered that moment vividly. It was one of the times when I had been visited by the shadow, of whom I had yet to learn the real identity. All I knew was that he had helped me on several occasions, most recently by warning me about the Harvester in the very same park we were standing in.

But the image of the strange mist wasn't what made my bones cold. In the photo, I was holding a spark of fire in my hand. The last time I had seen this picture was in the janitor's home before rescuing Jen. I thought I'd got all the pictures of us out of there, and I had burned them all in my room. Apparently, I had missed one. A very revealing one at that.

Stupid girl!

I stuffed the picture in my pocket.

Paddock nodded at me. "So you see, I know what you are."

If he judged me on account of holding fire in my hand, he might think I was a Sorceress, but I didn't want to correct him. Not yet, at least.

"And what? You want money? You've got the wrong girl." I studied him as the cold of my skin was slowly replaced by the fire growing in my veins. "You want to turn me over to a Harvester instead, perhaps?"

He shook his head. "Nothing like that. I've had this picture for weeks, and I haven't told a soul. All I want is your help."

Jen clasped her hand with mine, killing the small flame that had gathered in my palm without me even realising it. "Very well," she said. "You tell us what you need help with, and we'll decide what to make of it. But I warn you, this girl is packing some serious powers, and I'm not some obedient lapdog either."

Paddock looked from Jen and back to me, his eyes practically glowing as he turned the flashlight upwards. "You're both Mags?" He goggled at me. "Powers, as in plural?"

I shrugged.

Paddock shook himself, then lowered the flashlight again, leaving the three of us in the dim reflection of the beam. "Here's the gist of it. My partner was killed in September, about two weeks before the case we worked on your campus. It was apparently this kid who done it. They got in a fight when the kid supposedly tried to run, and the kid managed to stab my partner, Warren.

"As it turns out, the kid was found dead a bit later, drifting face down in the Thames. That means there's no one but another officer to verify the story of how Warren was killed. And this copper's not exactly a reliable kind of guy.

"So, before this, Warren was investigating our station on his own time. I had no idea until I found his notes. He left me a letter I was to open upon his death, which told me where to find everything. Guess he knew he was treading on dangerous ground. The rest of his stuff had clearly been searched, and most of his other files were confiscated."

Paddock took a deep breath before diving back into his story. "I didn't really think much of it, but it seemed important enough to keep hidden, so I took the files and a couple of other things from the compartment, then so much happened I almost forgot about it. A week after his death, I was assigned a new partner. You'll remember Fernsby? He's no longer my partner, though. Then there were the abductions and murders on your campus.

"Anyway, there's been some strange reports and shootouts lately, but anyone asking questions is more or less muzzled."

Jen held one hand up. "I'm sorry. I don't quite follow."

"I think I'm following. Kind of," I said. "Brendan and I were just talking about the rising crime rates the other night. Something is definitely up, and the MagX is most likely a big part of it."

Paddock's eyes shifted. He looked nothing like the man who had first come to interrogate me. If anything, he looked scared.

I gave him a slight smile for encouragement. "Go on."

"So," he muttered. "This is going to sound really weird, but Warren was a Mag—a Shifter."

"A wolf?" Jen asked, suddenly more agitated.

"Eh, no. He shifted into an eagle."

"Awesome."

"I suppose. I don't know. He was my partner and a good friend. As I said, though, I had almost forgotten about his stuff until a couple of days ago. Fernsby killed a girl, for no apparent reason. He said she attacked him, but the girl was tiny, and her records show no signs of aggression. Or they didn't when I first looked at them, but looks like someone has changed them. The entire situation is peculiar, to say the least. She was a skater, and her shirt had a specific emblem on it, depicting a sword, which reminded me of something." Paddock dug into his pockets again, then presented a plastic bag. "It's a bandana. What made me think of it was that the emblem was the same as the girl wore."

Jen waved her hand at the bag. "Give it."

Paddock didn't move.

"You should give it to her," I said.

He stared at me for a moment before he gave the bag to Jen. She opened the Ziplock and held it up to her nose. A couple of sniffs later, she screwed her head up, closed the bag and handed it to Paddock.

"Goblin," she announced.

"A what now?" Paddock asked.

"That thing belonged to a Goblin. I'm absolutely positive."

As far as I knew, there were a few Goblins still in existence. Mum even worked with a couple of them. There were probably other races out there who were still hiding as well, though the Goblins had managed to stay well under the radar when the rest of the Magicals were outed. Perhaps their time of hiding was coming to an end, too? Their powers weren't especially active, so I wasn't sure what use their blood would be if someone made MagX from it. It probably wouldn't sell much once the Harvesters' customers learned about the limitations of Goblin blood.

Paddock dipped his head. "Thank you. I suspected it came from a Mag. What I have learned so far has led me to believe that there are those in my department, if not in the entire force, who are working to hand over Mags to Harvesters—most likely for a hefty wad of cash —or worse, to downright execute them. I look over my shoulder every day, as if I've come too close to the truth or something. What I do know, is that this isn't what I signed up for."

"Have you told your boss about your suspicions?" I asked, not quite able to wrap my head around what he was saying.

"Can't trust anyone. That's why I contacted you. I know you had more to do with helping to solve the case of the missing girls than you've let on, and I don't know any other Mags. I figured you might have resources I don't. Besides, I don't think you'll talk about this, as it could expose yourself."

This was insane. How were we supposed to help with this? Still, if the police were targeting Mags, we were all hip-deep in trouble. And, he was right about trusting me to be quiet about my Fae persuasion.

"We'll help whichever way we can," I said, to my own surprise.

"Damned right we will," Jen chimed in.

"Not sure how we can help, though, but if you can get us everything you have from Warren's files, I'll see if I can dig up something. And I promise to be discreet about it."

"Right now, I don't have a choice but to trust you," he replied. "I don't think I have to tell you how much trouble you'll be in if you misuse that trust."

"You don't," I said. "And I—we won't."

Sticking his hand down yet another pocket, he

proceeded to hand me a small flip phone. "Non-traceable," he murmured. "I'll make contact soon."

The large officer walked away into the thicket on the opposite side of where we had entered, looking like he carried the weight of the world upon his shoulders. He probably felt like it, too, if he was working against his own colleagues. A small beam of light shone a distance away before Jen and I started the walk back to campus.

My mind was turning. If we couldn't trust the police to be on our side, then what?

# FIVE

My alarm was not aware of my desire to sleep in and churned out the far too happy tune I still hadn't changed. I grabbed my phone and started browsing through the various alarm signals, eventually settling on one that I thought wouldn't annoy me quite as much.

6.35. I had a lecture at 9.15 and was in no hurry. I couldn't sleep, though, so I got up and had a quick shower. Standing in the living room, with the other girls fast asleep, I noticed how big the flat felt—especially since Duncan wasn't here either. Maybe I should raise the issue of getting a couple more tenants. My problem with that, however, was that I didn't want anyone else living here. With Jen and Charlie—and Duncan, I guess—I felt safe. They all knew what I was, and I had no reason to hide it around them. If two strangers moved in, I would have to go through the whole process all over again, with no guarantees I would get the same approval from anyone new.

In the fridge, I found my usual yoghurt and went to the cupboard to get my muesli. I stopped. Not today, I thought, and decided to surprise the girls with a proper breakfast instead. Charlie usually had a bowl of cereal while Jen—well, it depended on whether she had slept in her bed the night before, or if she had been out hunting. Gross.

Popping the yoghurt back in the fridge, I grabbed the egg carton—happy to find there were still four left. Jen's old but still usable bacon strips lay in a plastic wrapping, and wouldn't you know—there was that black pudding Charlie had planned to have for dinner.

Half an hour or so later, I knocked on Jen's door. "Jeannine?" I whispered.

It never ceased to amaze me how she could be aeons away in a dream one second, only to look eager and awake the very next. Her icy blue eyes sparkled with joy and curiosity from under her duvet. I had to bite my lip to keep the laughter inside.

"What's up, honey?" she said as she stretched her arms and inched her head up onto the pillow.

"You know, if you had a tail, you'd wag it now," I replied, losing the fight against the giggle.

"Like this?" She pulled her silk shorts down half an inch and turned her back to me. From her lower back, a white, furry tail protruded and shook vigorously from side to side. The next second, it retracted into her skin, vanishing before my eyes.

"Jen!" I gasped. "That's—that's—"

"Cute? Sexy? Hot?"

"Yeah, sure. Those were the words I was looking for." I rolled my eyes. "Breakfast is ready, freak!"

"Really?" She sniffed the air. "Eggs, bacon, beans, and what, black pudding?"

"As I said, freak."

She laughed. "I'll be there in two."

I went to wake Charlie. When I knocked on her door, however, there was no reply. I knocked again. Then a little harder.

"Charlie? You hungry?"

"Humph?"

"I've made breakfast."

"No, thanks."

I opened the door and inserted my head. "Eggs on toast, bacon—the works. Come on, Char, we've got lots to tell you."

"Humph."

"Please?"

"Fine," she muttered.

I closed the door and went back to the kitchen. Although I hadn't exactly jumped into my alter ego of the French chef, the result was way more than our usual spread of cereal and yoghurt. The slices of black pudding were a tad overcooked, but I was quite pleased with the eggs. Sunnyside up and all.

Jen had already grabbed a piece of toast and poured maple syrup over it.

"Slept home all night?" I asked.

"Yup. Is there more bacon?"

"Nope. We need to go shopping. We're out of bread

and eggs, too. And I kinda snagged Charlie's black pudding."

"This is awesome, Red," she said between two mouthfuls. "I was famished." She stabbed a slice of the pudding and devoured it, smiling and winking at me. "You're hired!"

"I can't promise this every morning, I'm afraid. Didn't feel like running today, is all."

She nodded slowly. "I hear you."

Behind her, Charlie shuffled towards us, still in her PJs and her unicorn slippers. The contrast between her and Jen's mood was obvious. She yawned and sat down.

"Coffee?" I suggested.

"Sure." Charlie's voice was clipped.

I tried to meet her eyes, but failed, so I poured instead. "Milk?"

"Black." She grabbed the mug with both hands.

Not wanting to bug her too much this early, I left her alone. Jen, however, had no plans to let this pass.

"Come on, Charlie. Look at the feast Ru has prepared for us. It's great, no? She even lit the candles."

Charlie shrugged and grabbed a slice of toast from the wicker basket.

"Want some jam? Bacon?" I tried to sound cheerful, but by now irritation had crept into my voice.

Charlie reached across the table to get the jar of jam that stood right in front of me. She spread two table-spoons' worth of strawberry on her toast and took a bite. Not a word.

"Really? Nothing?" Jen had clearly had enough. "You don't think it's a bit—?"

"I think it was bad form to leave me behind yesterday, that's what I think." Charlie slammed the toast down onto the plate and stood to leave. She looked at me with tears in her eyes. "And yes, thanks for breakfast. I'm just not hungry."

"Sit down, please?" My voice trembled.

She hesitated. "I'll have some later. Thanks again." She went back to her room.

I looked at Jen, who was fuming. I put my hand on her shoulder. "Don't. I'll talk to her once she's simmered down."

Jen drew a long, hard breath. "Fine. But don't let her off the hook, ok?"

I smiled and nodded.

"I think I'll go for a walk after all," Jen said. "Thank you so much for breakfast. It was perfect."

She hugged me and kissed both my cheeks before dancing back to her room.

Although I was anxious to straighten things with Charlie, another thought had crept into my head. I finished my toast and emptied my glass of orange juice. I made a mental note of adding real oranges to the shopping list, instead of the concentrated version. Rather than clearing the table—Charlie could do that when, or if, she ate more later—I went to get my phone from the nightstand. A quick search on the Uni app provided me with Professor Kaine's number.

*Professor, would it be ok if I visited you at your office or lab later? I have a couple of questions. Ruby Morgan.*

I wasn't sure if he had stored my number, but it felt awkward signing the text message anyway.

His reply came after only a minute. I wasn't surprised, he had been up early on Saturday, too.

*Of course. I am in my office until noon, then lunch and then at my lab from about 1.30. When can I expect you?*

*Crap!* I had a lecture at 2.15 in the afternoon. I wanted to see him in his lab. For a second, I considered skipping the lecture but thought better of it. If I began skipping class every time I thought I had better things to do, I'd never graduate.

*11.30 ok? I won't keep you long.*

*Excellent, I look forward to it.*

"Later, sweetie," chirped Jen as she left. She looked like a million quid, her hair and makeup done to professional levels in what, ten minutes? Of course, it helped that she was totally supermodel gorgeous to begin with.

"See ya," I replied, looking back at my phone. I sent a text to Brendan, hoping he was in a better mood than yesterday. I had cancelled our date, yet I was the one feeling brushed off. It bugged me that I was nervous about his reply. "Get a grip, silly!" I whispered and sent the text.

*Good morning! Hope you've slept well. Give me a*
*ring if you want to hook up, ok?*

I switched the sound off, even though Charlie probably wouldn't hear the chime when Brendan replied.
Or if she did, she would more likely ignore it, sulking
about last night. If only I could make her understand it
was for her own good.

I glanced at her door, wanting to go talk to her. But
no, she needed more time to cool off. And maybe, so
did I.

Instead, I grabbed one of the wax candles, went
back to my room and closed the door carefully. For a
second, I contemplated turning the lock but decided to
not take the chance on Charlie hearing the click. I put
the candle on my desk, dropped to the floor and
stretched my arm under the bed to pull out my suitcase. Small pockets lined the inside, and in one of them
I found the thing Mum had said she was sure I would
need at some point. Well, I did, but not at all for the
purpose she thought.

I turned on the desk lamp and sat by the desk. The
little plastic box was about the size of a credit card. In
fact, as I now examined it for the first time, it even said
so on the lid: "Credit card sized sewing kit for
travellers."

For the life of me, I could not remember the last time
I had sewn anything. Maybe way back in primary school.
It simply had never interested me. Still, I had to admit,
the sewing kit was kind of neat. There was a foldable

pair of scissors, a cylinder with four different coloured threads and a strangely shaped, thin metal thing—I had no idea what it was. There was also an assortment of buttons and a small, tube-shaped plastic container with a tiny lid. It was no bigger than the cap of a marker pen. I flipped open the lid and found what I was looking for.

Needles and pins.

When I emptied the small container, carefully so as to not have any of the needles drop off the desk, a second thought emerged. The box itself could be useful.

I chose one of the sewing needles, and put all the others back in the kit box, keeping the tiny tube.

When I was eight or nine years old, Dad had once used a safety pin to get a tiny splinter out of my toe. He used a match to sterilise the tip before he went into surgery, as he called it. Mum scolded him when we came home, saying he should know that it wasn't a safe way to sterilise a needle. Dad said he didn't insert the pin very far, and that the splinter wasn't deep in my veins or anything. Besides, he argued, the flame was way better than not sterilising at all, to which Mum had sort of agreed.

I held the sewing needle over the candle's flame, hoping it would be hot enough for what I needed to do. If I had more control over my firepower, I guess I could have conjured a much hotter flame myself, but chances were I would set my room ablaze if I tried.

In my bathroom, I rinsed the little plastic tube with hot water and soap, finishing it off with a Q-tip I had dipped in nail polish remover. I used another Q-tip, also dipped in the same solvent, to wipe the soot off the tip of the needle. Then I pinched the tip of my little finger and pricked the reddened fingertip with the needle. A small drop of blood floated up over my skin.

I held my fingertip over the small plastic container and pushed a few drops of blood into it. Finally, I pressed the lid back on and went back to the kitchen. There, I wrapped the makeshift blood vial tightly in cling film, and a thick layer of aluminium foil just to be sure.

A quick glance out the window told me I'd better put on my raincoat, which was perfect. The large pockets would both conceal and protect the package. I slipped into my room again to get it and dropped the container into one of the pockets. When I was out in the hallway, ready to go, I knocked on Charlie's door again.

"I'm off, Charlie. You wanna eat alone, it's all yours."

No reply.

*Fine!*

I left.

On my way to class, I checked my phone. Not a word from Brendan. What was up with him? This simply wouldn't do. First Charlie and now Brendan. And neither of them would even discuss it? Well, two could play at that game. Or three, or whatever. I was pissed.

The lecture was probably way more interesting than I managed to grasp. My thoughts were not at all focused on Wharton and his meandering on about

"Getting your message across". The irony was not lost on me.

I fought away the angry thoughts of Brendan and Charlie and focused on what Paddock had told me yesterday. "Too close to the truth," he had said. Basically, he claimed his old partner had been killed because he was about to bust the corrupt coppers. Could it really be true?

On the screen up front, Wharton showed a picture of a guy riding his mountain bike down a steep trail. I had no idea what he was on about. Why had I picked a seat in the middle of the row? I wasn't one to sneak out during lectures, but now I wanted to.

Wharton eventually finished with a slide that was full of text. I tried to read it, something about remembering and using the simple rules he had gone through in today's lecture. And here I was, thinking the message was that one should keep things short and to the point.

When I had read maybe halfway through the slide, the words started fading away. In the middle of the screen, three of the words remained. Ok, that was actually a little clever. The words had been part of a sentence about '—that the principle of less is more should be your guideline—'

Now, only 'less is more' remained on the screen.

"You see, all those other words said the exact same as these three. So, why bother with more than three?"

He looked like he expected a standing ovation, but save for a few claps, most of us were just eager to get on with our day. Including me. I had tried to make some notes on my laptop but realised I would need more than the random lines I had jotted down. Luckily, Wharton's presentation was available for download in Canvas, so I figured I'd be all right.

I slung the bag over my shoulder and headed for the door. The library was in the adjacent building, and I found myself a quiet corner. I opened my laptop and launched my web browser. After a few minutes, I had found a few articles using search terms related to what Paddock had told me.

"Miss Morgan?"

I looked up. "Professor Kaine," I whispered.

"I have rearranged my schedule. My lunch appointment was cancelled, so I thought I might do some other tasks. When I saw you, I thought I'd ask if we should meet earlier? If you're not busy, of course."

He glanced at my screen. "Three dead in a police shooting, Twickenham." He nodded. "Yes, I remember that. Nasty business."

"I—I'm doing research for a story in the Whisper," I said, not sure how much I wanted to share with him.

"The Whisper, yes. I remember when it came only weekly, two or three pages stapled in the upper left corner."

"It's come a bit further now," I said. "I've been working there for a few weeks. It's fast-paced and a new way of getting the news out quicker."

"Very impressive. I must admit I still prefer the smell and ink of the old newspapers myself. Not that I don't like computers, mind you, but the Sunday Times really does go better with tea and biscuits."

I smiled. "I won't argue with that."

"You wanted to ask me something?"

We were alone in this section, but I lowered my voice anyway. "Yes, but not here."

"Let's go to my office," he said.

"Could we perhaps go to your lab instead, Professor?"

"Certainly." He raised his dark eyebrows. "Now you've intrigued me."

---

I had visited Mum at work a few times over the years and was used to intricate lab equipment. Not that there was a lab at the clinic, but at least they had lots of glasses, vials, test tubes and Petri dishes to accompany a few machines with monitors and bleeps.

The room Kaine showed me into, however, was on another level entirely. It was truly the mad professor version of a lab. I half expected to be greeted by a short, hump-backed creature with an eye-patch and a Russian accent. The only thing missing was the yellow and green vapour clouds rising from a suspicious-looking liquid boiling over a Bunsen burner. Somehow, I bet Kaine could produce it if I asked him.

"So, Miss Morgan, what was it you wanted to ask me?"

"It's more of a 'show you' thing, really," I said and retrieved the foil and plastic-wrapped package from my coat pocket.

My phone was in the same pocket, but I resisted the temptation to check for word from Brendan.

"I'm not sure if it's something you can do, but I'd like you to have a look at this," I continued, and unwrapped the small plastic container. "Can you tell me about the contents?"

His glasses hung on a chain around his neck, and the old professor put them on, leaning forward to examine the tube. He put his finger under the lid, sent me a quick look over his glasses and, when I nodded, he flicked the lid open.

"At first glance, it looks like blood. Fresh enough that it hasn't started to coagulate yet."

"It's blood, yes. That's about all I know."

"Then we'll have to pretend I know more," Kaine said with a small laugh. "Is it ok if I run some tests?"

"I was sort of hoping you would," I said.

Kaine used a small glass pipette to extract a drop of the dark purple blood, which he then dripped into a glass tube. He closed the plastic tube, carefully wrapped the package again and handed it to me. I slipped it back in my pocket and followed him to a white appliance next to a large glass cupboard.

"This is a centrifuge," he said, tapping the box. "The newest of its kind, capable of separating blood far quicker than the industry standard versions."

Not sure what reaction he wanted from me, I tried to look moderately impressed.

"Let's see what the boys at JC Pharmaceuticals have made, shall we?" Kaine gave the container a quick shake.

At first, I didn't understand, but then he pointed at the logo on the side of the machine.

"I've worked closely with the men and women in their R&D division up in Stevenage, and contributed to the development of this prototype."

If I hadn't been so focused on the blood itself, I might have understood what an achievement that had to be.

"Oh, listen to me, tooting my own horn like an idiot."

He opened the rubber cap on the glass tube with my blood in it and poured a clear liquid into the tube. "A special gel that helps the separation process," he explained, before placing the glass in one of the holes in the centrifuge. He closed the lid and tapped the touch screen on the front. "There, now it'll whirr and do its job for a couple of minutes."

"I'll just check my phone," I said. "See if there's anything new on the message boards."

I turned, retrieved my phone and let my fingerprint unlock the screen. Two messages in Canvas, one email, and exactly zero texts from Brendan. Cursing myself for checking, I shoved the phone back in my pocket, somehow present minded enough to choose the one without the blood.

"Bad news?" Kaine asked.

"Not really. More like no news from someone I'd expected to hear from."

The almost silent engine in the centrifuge stopped. "It really is a whole new world for chemists." Kaine smiled. "Imagine how much it will mean to trauma victims and emergency units to save up to twenty-five or thirty minutes when they need test results. This will save lives, prin—primarily."

"Primarily?"

"Eh ... yes," he said. "I think the primary deployment of these units should be in emergency treatment. Well, let's see what we have here."

He lifted the glass and held it up to the light, showing four separate layers of liquid. One layer was clear at the top, the next milkier, followed by a thin red layer. Underneath the red was a tiny, almost invisible layer of blue liquid.

"Interesting," said Kaine. He inserted a white paper strip, and when he pulled it out, the layers were drawn on the paper—like a printed version of what was in the tube.

"Also an invention of the JC Pharma geniuses. In fact, sometimes what they do up there is magic in itself."

He walked down to the biggest microscope I had ever seen and put the paper strip between two glass plates. Dropping his glasses down to his chest again, he leaned forward and looked into the eyepieces.

"It's magic blood, all right," he said. "Not pure, but quite potent."

Tell me about it. For a second, I feared he might be able to see what powers it contained. That would really freak him out. Or me, for that matter.

"How can you tell it's magic?" I asked, trying to remember what I had read in a Wikipedia article a while back. Something about the ratio between the blood cells.

"Pure magical blood has about one thousand blue blood cells to every white. This is quite rare, however, as most Magicals nowadays are descendants of mixed parents."

*Like me*, I wanted to say. I had never been closer to revealing my Fae heritage to any human, apart from Charlie, of course. It was a good feeling to believe I could trust Kaine.

"This one, however, has about three hundred blue cells to every white. A half-blood, one could say. Although most Magicals' blood has lower cell counts, this looks pretty standard for a half-blood."

I knew about the half-blood issue, at least, but I had to admit it stung a little to be described as 'pretty standard'. Ironic, as all my life I had wanted to be normal, like the other kids at school. Moreover, I had kind of hoped for some real answers. The Harvesters who had kidnapped Jen said my blood was special. And though I already knew I wasn't anything out of the ordinary, I had to check. Their intel was clearly wrong.

But Kaine's numbers still puzzled me. "Half? Wouldn't that mean like, five hundred blue cells?"

"The maths is a bit skewed," said Kaine. "It's more of a logarithmic scale than a linear one."

"Maths was never my forte, I'm afraid. But ok, if this is blood from a half-blood Mag, could—?"

"Please, Miss Morgan. I have far too much respect for our guests here on Earth to use that term. Let's give them the courtesy of calling them Magical beings, shall we?" He didn't change his voice or expression, but his tone conveyed this meant something to him. Something important.

"Our ... guests?"

"Why, indeed," he said, smiling wryly. "I have always viewed Magicals as an enrichment to this godforsaken planet. Unfortunately, the majority of humans seem to disagree with me on the matter."

"At least, if that crazy Colburn is the benchmark," I said, immediately regretting it.

Kaine laughed. "Yes, he is quite the character. A brilliant scientist with an impeccable record of helping the needy and poor of the world. But yes, I don't agree with his views on Magicals, neither the religious nor the political angle."

I'm not sure what came over me. A warm, kind and safe sensation flowed through my body, and without knowing it, I held my hands in front of me. Palms up. Two tiny balls of fire hovered an inch above my hands.

My gaze found Kaine's eyes, expecting to see shock or fear. The fireballs reflected in his pupils, making them appear bright orange and glowing. He tilted his head slightly, and one corner of his mouth drew up.

What the hell was I doing? I closed my fists, forcing the fireballs back into wherever they came from—somewhere inside me, I guessed.

"I—I'm so sorry, Professor," I said, my voice choked. "I'm so very sorry!"

I ran out of the lab, down the hall towards the stairway. I'm not sure how I managed to descend it without falling flat on my face, but soon I found myself sprinting in the pouring rain away from the Chem

Building. My face was soaking wet from the rain, but also from the tears that flowed like rivers from my eyes.

It had felt so right. It had felt so ... safe.

I didn't stop until I crashed into our flat. My boots left muddy footprints in the hallway, and I almost slipped as I tore my door open. Being a half-blood Fae, flying was not one of my powers, but I came pretty damned close as I threw myself on the bed.

It had felt so right. And safe.

Wasn't it?

# SIX

I STOOD BY THE STEPS TO CRAYDON AND TEXTED Brendan. Again. When I still had no response a couple of minutes later, I turned on my heels and stomped off. It wasn't like him not to respond. I had wanted to talk to Charlie about what went down this morning at breakfast, and about my visit with Kaine, but I couldn't deal with her sulkiness right now. And now Brendan was giving me the silent treatment on top of it all? He had some explaining to do.

*Grow up, Ru!*

It was silly of me to get this upset, and he probably had some reasonable explanation. The events of the past few days weighed on me, and although we had not decided on what we were, I needed him. As a friend, if nothing else. I couldn't tell him anything about Paddock or Kaine, but he wasn't one to pry, which was one of the things I liked about him. One of many. Right now, though, I was riling myself up, all but slamming my fists to my chest in a roar of frustration. He'd better have a damn good reason for his behaviour or lack thereof.

Rounding the corner, I quickened my steps, striding against the headwind. A leaf blew in front of my eyes, and I shook it off like an annoyed cat coming in from the rain.

Ealing House was a bit bigger than Craydon, though still smaller than Raven Court. Each flat had eight rooms, as opposed to our six, and the standard of the rooms was a lot better than ours. Thus, the rent was a lot higher, which was why I didn't live in Ealing. Mum helped me with living costs, but combined, we could barely afford me living on campus at all. And yet she had agreed that I shouldn't stay in the cheapest accommodation, Westerly Court, where twenty-four students shared separate loos and showers. It would have cost both of us a lot less, but it seemed Mum valued my privacy even more than I did.

I walked straight across the small circular garden in front of Ealing, then rang the doorbell of number five.

A girl opened. "Yes?"

"Brendan home?" I asked, pushing past her before she could reply, then rushing down the hallway to room six, which oddly enough was the same number as mine. My fist found the door with great determination.

"Just a moment," Brendan shouted on the other side. There was a short click of a lock before the door swung open.

"Ru—"

"Save it. You want to tell me why you've decided to be an ass?" I crossed my arms, taking a stance befitting for a commander in the army. "Are you still pissed I had to cancel on you yesterday? I mean, I did tell you, and you seemed fine about it."

"I—"

"Where do you come off acting like that? I needed you, and—"

"Ruby!" Brendan interrupted, stepping aside to wave a hand into the room.

My mouth clenched shut. He wasn't alone. A girl was sitting on his bed, and a pink suitcase lay half open on the floor beside it. Did he have a girlfriend he had failed to tell me about? My anger flared up. I balled my hands, trying to stop the oncoming surge of energy boiling forth in my veins. I wanted to torch the place, burn that stupid pink suitcase, along with Brendan and everything else. Maybe not Brendan, but still.

He shook his head wildly, clearly picking up on what was upsetting me. "Ruby," he said again. "This is Teagan."

I exhaled slowly, my cheeks burning, and not from the fire that was settling back into a dormant state. The embarrassment was overwhelming.

"Oh," I muttered, staring at Brendan's sister. My shoulders slumped. "You must think I'm completely mental."

Tegan glanced at me, and for the first time, I really looked at her. It was strange to look into the girly version of Brendan's eyes. Unlike his, hers were veiled with tears.

Brendan sighed. "Since you're here, and everyone is already upset, you might as well come in."

At this point, I'd rather run back out, but as invited, I stepped inside before Brendan shut the door behind me.

"I'm interrupting something," I said.

"You are," Brendan retorted. "But I'm sorry I didn't reply. It's just that Teagan showed up yesterday, and we've had some things to sort out. I didn't mean to blow you off."

I sat on the chair by his desk while Brendan dumped down beside his sister, who had yet to say a word to me.

"Teagan, this is Ruby, my friend. Or something." A small dimple formed as he gave me a short smile. "She doesn't usually shout this much."

Teagan blew her nose into a tissue, then tossed it on top of the bin, which was nearly full of already used ones. Then she held my gaze. Her dark brown hair brushed her shoulders, and her face was the pretty equivalent to Brendan's handsomeness. If I didn't know any better, I'd say they were twins. There were, however, some more delicate features of her face that made her look younger than him, even though I knew she was two years older. She had, according to Brendan, dropped out in the middle of her bachelor's studies last spring to run a hotel on the Sun Coast with her boyfriend. Her tan, or rather lack of it, did not tell a tale of hours in the sun, though.

"You're dating my brother?" Teagan asked, not waiting for a reply. "Then you should know better than to barge in on him."

I nodded. She was making a point, and though I

could have gone into a debate with her about the dating, she didn't look like she was up for much of anything.

"He's very loyal." Teagan ruffled Brendan's hair, then bore her eyes into me again. "Especially to his family."

I sat at the edge of my seat, but didn't say anything, afraid Brendan might throw me out. Now that I had sat down, I didn't want to leave anymore; I wanted to know what was going on. Why was she here and not in Spain, for starters?

Brendan removed Teagan's hand from the top of his head. "Can I tell Ruby? She already knows what Ollie is." He smiled at me, a small but tender smile that made my skin tingle.

Teagan frowned at him and wiped the tears on her cheeks. "Sure. Why not. Can't get any worse."

I was pretty sure it could, but I kept that to myself.

"You remember I told you about Teagan's boyfriend, Oliver?" Brendan asked. "Well, as it turns out, there was more to the story than I knew when I told you about it. He still conned our parents, though it seems it was all Teagan's idea. He was running away from a group of Harvesters, and Teagan figured they could borrow the money and pay our parents back later." He shook his head. "However stupid that was, the money wasn't enough, and a few days ago, they came for him."

"They kidnapped him," Teagan cried. "They tased him, shackled him, and took him away. I only escaped because he spent all his energy creating a magical diversion, tricking them into thinking I wasn't there. It gave me a chance to hide, but there were three of them, and he didn't have enough energy left to fool them all. He saved me, and now he's gone."

Well, bugger, this added to my very long list of troubles.

Teagan sniffled. "When they last took him, they brought him someplace north of London, though he escaped before they got to their destination. I have to find him!"

I knew better than anyone how dangerous Harvesters could be, and it might already be too late, but no one deserved to be kidnapped and have their blood drained against their will. Perhaps the Harvesters who took Oliver were a little more careful than the ones who had taken Jen and the other girls. If so, then maybe he was still alive.

"So, you see," Brendan said, "I've had my hands full."

I sighed. "I can see that. Whatever you need, don't hesitate to ask. I'd like to help find him."

Teagan slanted her head at me, no doubt sizing me up to decide if I would be of any use at all. "I suppose it wouldn't hurt."

"I study journalism," I said, as if that gave me some merit. "I've got access to newspaper files as well as some powerful search engines and databases. If you can gather everything you know and send it to me, then I'll try to see if I can find something that might help. I don't know if I can, but I'll do my best."

She nodded and leaned her head on Brendan's shoulder.

He gave me an apologetic look, but I waved him off. "We'll talk again tomorrow?"

"I'll text you."

"You do that."

With a deep breath, I stood and exited Brendan's room. The wind outside had picked up again, but it didn't bother me anymore. I had too much on my mind. Mum had always warned me about the Harvesters, and I had known that they would be a threat, but this seemed to be much more organised than I had thought. They had the equipment to immobilise magic, to capture and drain people, and not only that, if you ran, they came after you. Would they have killed Teagan if they had found her? If so, they were willing to sacrifice humans, too.

And then there was the police. Paddock had said not to trust anyone, and I had thought him to be paranoid. Perhaps he wasn't after all. Besides, paranoia might be the right response in a situation like this. No Mag was safe, which meant Jen wasn't safe. I wasn't. And maybe Mum wasn't either, and she was all alone.

The hallway was dark as I trudged towards my room. I lingered outside Charlie's door for a moment, then decided I had nothing left to give. We would talk, just not now. Maybe things would look up in the morning, though I had my doubts.

# SEVEN

I YAWNED, FINISHED THE SPELLCHECK AND GLANCED AT the time. 5.52 am. The file on my laptop had started to blur into a mess of letters. I drew my breath, shook my head to regain focus, and closed the assignment. It wasn't due until 2 pm, but with everything that was going on, I had decided to work through the night to get ahead. I still had to write a piece for the Whisper about the upcoming election for the students' representative on the university board, but that would have to wait.

I uploaded the assignment paper to my Canvas account. It was good, though not great. Hopefully, it would get me a 2:1 grade, but that might be a stretch. In my mind, the 2:1 was an absolute target. Of course, the first obstacle was to pass at all, but I had something to prove. Mostly to myself. Also, I wanted Mum to know I could cope with juggling both uni, work, the Whisper and, as it turned out, a possible boyfriend. If Brendan was still interested after the stunt I'd pulled last night, that was.

As I had plenty more schoolwork to do, I slipped my laptop into my bag and dashed past Charlie coming from the kitchen in her PJs, a coffee mug in her hands. She stopped and turned after me as I went for the door.

"Later," I called. "I promise."

I wanted to talk to her, I really did, but my mind could only cope with so much. Right now, I needed to find my three predicaments for Mr Zhang's class and start working on my arguments. After that, I had to look for anything I could find about Harvesters north of London and do some digging into Ollie's past. I didn't have a lot to go on. Also, Paddock would likely get in touch soon, so I had to get started, or I might not find the time.

The sun was out, and though it was chilly, the wind had stilled. Maybe things would get better today. Not wanting to sit anywhere crowded, I found a bench by the entrance to the labyrinth garden, feeling as happy as I was surprised to be able to work outdoors this late in November. Wi-Fi reception on campus was pretty good, and the area was quiet this early. I opened my laptop as a squirrel darted across the ground and disappeared into the hedge. Seconds later, another squirrel followed its path. I blew into my hands and rubbed them together. My fingers would soon freeze to the point where I couldn't sit out there for too long. Perhaps not the brightest idea to work outside after all, though I was determined to enjoy the sunshine for as long as I could manage.

"Truth," I wrote before my mind shut down. It took me a while to sort out my thoughts as to what Mr Zhang might want from this assignment. I had just finished writing something half decent about respecting privacy when a familiar cane tapped the top of the screen.

"Miss Morgan." Kaine stared down at me. "You do like to get an early start. I admire that in someone as young as you. I bet if we're quiet enough, we could hear the snoring chorus of your fellow students."

I almost laughed, then remembered what I had done. My cheeks flared up, and my instincts told me to run again.

"Professor Kaine," I muttered, pressed save and slowly closed my laptop to place it back in my bag.

"I was wondering if I might have a moment?" he said.

"I—I'm really very busy."

He folded his hands on top of his cane, leaning towards me. "It will be worth your while."

Scrambling to my feet, I motioned towards Craydon. "Charlie is waiting for me."

"One should not tell lies, Miss Morgan." He tutted. "Though I understand why you think you ought to run. I promise it will all become clear to you if you will allow me a fraction of your time."

Why was he so persistent? I couldn't deal with another problem today, and Kaine knowing what I was, well, that was a can of worms I didn't want to get into. I started to walk off when the cane cut in front of me.

"Miss Morgan." Kaine's voice was deeper this time,

full of power and authority. "I cannot show you what you need to see out here in the open. But we both know that I know. And that little display of yours showed me that you do not have control over yourself. It is a dangerous thing in this world to not contain your powers when needed. I should know."

I paused and met his gaze. His silver-blue eyes looked both young and old at the same time, as if they were filled with fire and wisdom. There was something about him. Yesterday, I had felt safe in his presence, and his words had soothed me. It was my own fault that I messed up. Would he betray me to the Harvesters? I didn't think he would. And what had he just said? He should know?

"All right," I said. "I'll text Jen first to let her know that I'm with you. In case she starts to worry."

That should get the message across. He wouldn't hurt me if people knew he was the last person to see me. A simple precaution, which I most likely didn't need. It was pure paranoia, but I had already decided that paranoia was to be my approach going forward. The ordeal with the janitor had taught me that anyone could be a wolf in sheep's clothing, and the Harvester in the park on Saturday morning hadn't exactly vanished from my mind either.

"You're a smart girl, Miss Morgan." Kaine gestured with his cane, and I followed in his steps. We passed by Ealing Court, and I couldn't help but look for Brendan. He wasn't outside, though, and was probably still in bed.

Focus, Ru!

Kaine led me behind Ealing and past one of the lecture halls, proceeding by the accommodation house for the lecturers, past Raven Court and beyond. My breath caught in my throat as I realised where we were headed. The entrance to the tunnels, which led to the boiler room I had blown up—literally—was closed off with more blue tape than it had been the first time I had trespassed.

Kaine lifted the tape, beckoning for me to follow. I hesitated, turning the ring on my finger while sending a thought to my dad. I had no idea why I did that, but I supposed it helped calm me when I was nervous.

"Do not linger," Kaine said. He flicked his fingers at the sealed-off doors, and the padlock disintegrated into dust in seconds.

What on Earth or Avalon? Did he use magic? My lips spread out into an involuntary smile. I dipped underneath the tape, and we stepped inside the dark tunnel.

"We could use some light," he murmured.

I grinned. With no one else watching, I drew on the power always present in my veins. It took me some time, however, as my firepower and I had not been able to get properly acquainted yet. I wasn't about to have another accidental explosion that could very well kill us both. A ball of fire erupted in my palm, emitting a dim light, which eased visibility as we traversed further, not stopping again until we stood on top of the rubble of what had once been the boiler room.

"There are a few torches on the wall." Kaine tilted his chin at one torch after another, making six in total.

Torches? That was completely medieval. I stifled a laugh and shrugged.

"Sure," I said, then sent a tendril of flame to each of them. The torches lit up as the fire got a hold, the room bright enough on its own for me to kill the fireball in my hand.

"Very good. And no explosions this time."

That made me pause. "Wait. How did you know?"

He circled me, his cane tracing the blocks of cement as he went. Slowly, a steady stream of smoke surrounded us as the rubble disintegrated in much the same way as the padlock. Soon, we were standing on what looked like an arena, the floor level, though covered in ash.

My eyes widened. What was he? An Elementalist? Whatever he was, he was clearly a Magical. He had such a calm control of his powers that there was no way he could be high on MagX.

He stopped in front of me, his posture straight, too straight for an old man. "When you asked for my help, I got curious, so I had a look at what you found in the archives and discovered you had printed the blueprints for the tunnels. Not my proudest moment, I must admit, but I followed you. I waited outside until I heard the blast. The rest I could piece together easily enough."

The night I had become a live bomb was vivid in my mind. There were still things about what had happened that I didn't fully understand, however. Perhaps Kaine could help me figure it out?

"So, you already knew what I was? You knew the blood I had you test was mine, too, didn't you?" I asked.

"It wasn't my secret to tell, Miss Morgan."

I tilted my head at him. "Call me Ruby, please. I think we're past the Miss Morgan phase."

He chuckled. "Then you should call me Gabriel."

Gabriel, I mused. Gabriel Kaine was as biblical as names went. Not a common name for a Magical, and he didn't strike me as particularly angelic. He did have this guardian kind of look about him, though.

I presented my hand, and we shook. "Pleased to meet you, Gabriel. Now, why exactly are we here?"

"Your little magical display in my lab made me realise you might need some, shall we say, guidance. I'm not sure why your mother never taught you control. It is, after all, something that needs to be learned."

I stepped back and frowned. "My mum taught me a lot of things. I am perfectly in control of my healing, and usually of my force fields. It's those weird new powers I struggle with."

"I apologise, I meant no offence to your mother." He tapped the pommel of his cane with two fingers. "But what do you mean by weird new powers?"

"Lately I've been able to—" I started, not sure how much to reveal. "Well, you saw the fireballs. Not your average Fae power, right?"

"Not at all. That explains so much and at the same time so little. No one gets new powers once they are fully developed. Magical powers are innate. You should have always had them."

My eyes widened. "What do you mean? I've had

them all along? Then why have I never used them before?"

"That is very peculiar, indeed."

I slid a finger over the ruby on my ring. "Did you see anything in my blood to indicate I have non-Fae powers?"

He shook his head. "No, but the nature of the magical powers is not visible in the blood. There is no pattern to the blood cells that we are aware of as yet. This is certainly a conundrum. There are only two explanations I can think of which could have caused these powers to show up now rather than before. One is that you somehow stole them, intentionally or not, from someone else."

"I didn't—"

He held one hand up. "The other, and the more likely scenario, is that the powers were disconnected from you. Bound, perhaps."

I shook my head. It didn't make sense. "How do you know so much?"

"I've been all over the world, Ruby. I do not have powers such as yours, and I cannot do all the things you can, but knowledge is power, too."

The revelations of what he was saying were too much to grasp, though there was one point he had made, which was something to take to heart.

"So, could you teach me control?"

If I could get a handle on these new powers, then maybe I stood a better chance against the Harvesters of the world. One could hope.

His eyes lit up, and that fire in them I had seen

before made him look young again. "Yes, Ruby. I believe I can. And this," he gestured outwards with his cane, "will be our training ground. It's secluded, and you can break whatever you want in here."

"Thank you, Prof—I mean, Gabriel. Truly."

He tilted his chin at me. "We'll find the time. In the mornings perhaps. You could combine it with your runs. This kind of training is very much like physical exercise. Besides, you did mention having a busy day."

We made our way outside and split up. He sauntered in the direction of the accommodation hall for lecturers, while I took the shortcut by Raven Court through the lilac archway. I didn't have any lectures to get to, but I did have a friend, with whom I needed to make amends. I had a couple of ideas on how to brighten her day as well. With my spirits uplifted, I picked up speed and ran all the way back to Craydon.

As I skipped up the steps, my phone vibrated in my pocket.

*Taking Teagan out for distractions today, but sent you an email with what we have. Hope to see you soon, milady. X*

I could feel myself practically beaming with joy as I danced into the hallway and crashed straight into Charlie.

# EIGHT

"I'm sorry!" I said, my words drowning in Charlie's exact same outburst.

We looked at each other for a couple of seconds, then exploded into fits of laughter and threw ourselves into an embrace. Slowly, we released one another, and I leaned back to look her in the eyes.

"I really am sorry, Char!"

"You and me both," she replied.

"Can we talk?"

"Yes, please," she said, with an over-the-top dramatic voice. "I've got about four seconds of patience left before I die. These last couple of days have been a total nightmare."

We went into the living room and sat in what had more or less become our reserved seats—me in the armchair and Charlie snuggled in the far end of the sofa.

"I was a spoiled brat yesterday," she said, fiddling with the string on her hoodie. "When you left, I snuck

out and ate a shitload of the delicious breakfast you'd
made, sobbing all through it."

"It must have gone cold by then."

"Worked for me." Her eyes were still downcast.
"You've got to cook it again sometime."

"I will," I said. "But let's get to the point, ok? What
happened was I got a call on Monday from PC
Paddock, one of the coppers that were here when
Ilyana disappeared, remember?"

"Why?" She looked up at me, eyebrows raised. "I
mean, yeah, I remember the police—think there were
three of them. But what did he want? Was it the nice
one, by the way?"

"Yes and no. When he was here, I thought he was
rude. He seemed to hate Mags, and his boss, DCI
Davies, even apologized to us for Paddock's
behaviour."

She snapped her fingers. "I remember that. It was
actually kinda cool. So, Paddock's not the nice one,
then."

"Turns out, he kind of is. I'll get to that. He asked
me to meet him in Richmond Park that night."

"Come again?"

I raised my hand. "That was my first thought as
well. But he said it was important, so I got curious. Also,
I asked Jen to go with me, for—"

Charlie gave a quick snort and a little shrug. "For
backup in case it was dangerous, I get it."

"Well, yes. I didn't want to take any chances."

"Way to make a girl feel utterly useless." The anger
had crept back into her eyes, and she threw her arms

up. "But hey, what good is a mere human when you have magic literally at your fingertips?"

At first, I wanted to tell her I was wrong, and that I should have included her, but that would be a lie.

I bit my lip, staring at her. "You know what? You're right," I said between gritted teeth. "We didn't want to take you with us because it could have been dangerous. And yes, it was my decision. For all I knew, it was a trick. A trap. Maybe Paddock had some deal with a Harvester, even. So, to be on the safe side, I brought Jen. And I deliberately left you behind for your own safety."

"Do you have any idea how condescending that sounds? Who the hell made you the master of my life? I am fully capable of looking after myself, thank you very much!"

"Oh, shut up, you fool," I blurted. "Don't you get it? Have you no clue how much I love you? How it would kill me if anything happened to you?"

I was shaking inside, and the last words came out at such a high, desperate pitch that I wasn't sure she could understand them.

Charlie said nothing, and I swallowed hard, quelling the rising fire inside. My gaze was locked on her as if I could force my desperation into her mind.

"I—" she muttered, lowering her gaze again. "I didn't think of it that way."

"No shit," I said under my breath.

To my horror, a tiny ball of fire had formed in my right hand. I concentrated hard and managed to retract it. I really needed Kaine's help controlling this.

"It's just—" Charlie began. She hesitated, looking

up at the ceiling as if the right words were up there. "I can't cope with being left out. And of course, you're right. What could my contribution be in a fight with policemen and Harvesters and shit?"

I drew a deep breath, collecting myself. "The way you've let me into your life has meant more to me than you can imagine. I've never had a friend like you. Ever!"

"My therapist will be thrilled," she said. "She has pushed so hard for me to have a close friend."

I had no idea she went to therapy. But then again, if one were to trust the magazines and bloggers, seeing a psychiatrist seemed to be the norm. Just a couple of weeks ago, I'd noticed a headline in The Times. You're not seeing a shrink? Are you crazy? I remembered smiling at the joke but skipping the article itself. Maybe I should go back and have a look.

"And now you have two friends," I said. "Plus Duncan."

"Yeah." She sniffled. "Donna will be over the moon."

"Donna?"

"Donnatella Moss. My therapist. I've been going for three years, nearly every week."

I wanted to ask why but didn't want to cross the line.

"Why?" Charlie winked at me.

"So, you read minds, do you?" I said, returning the wink.

"Not really, but it's normal to want to know, and you're simply too polite to ask. The short version—the diagnosis, so to speak—is fear of abandonment. The long version is—well, that's the long version, too, I guess. That, and the fear stemming from growing up more or less by myself."

"Oh?"

"I told you about my dad, didn't I? His tendency to view a can of beer as an aperitif and a bottle of vodka as the main course?"

I nodded, not wanting to interrupt her.

"He was my hero. I desperately wanted to be like him. His jokes, his brilliant mind, his stories. And the way he turned bedtime reading into our own kind of magic. There was this one story in particular, about a boy wizard and a school for wizards and witches. They never caught on, though. Guess the world didn't find books about wizards all that interesting, not with real magic all around. But Dad knew the author, so he got the whole set from her. Anyway, this boy wizard had a friend, a girl who was born with no magic at all, just like me. She ended up being one of the strongest of all the characters in the books, even though she wasn't a born Magical."

Her eyes lit up. The memories clearly had a special place in her heart. I glanced at the print on her homemade t-shirt. Don't let the Muggles bring you down. She wore it a lot, and I suspected it had something to do with those books she always talked about.

Charlie exhaled with a heavy puff. "At that time, Dad only drank beer. It made him funny, at least in my eyes. He wrote a couple of children's books himself. Got a nice contract for a whole series, in fact. Never got further than the second one, though. By then, he had fallen in love with the vodka."

"Oh, Charlie. That's terrible."

She shrugged. "I was ten when he stopped being my hero. I still loved him, mind you, but I had also begun loathing him for not being my hero anymore. He turned into this sorry sack of shit. When the book deal came, he quit his job. Said he'd make it big with the next volume. I asked why he didn't write it. 'You can't hurry art, Lotty,' was his standard response. I used to love that nickname. It lost its magic, one could say."

"What about your mum?"

"She tried, I guess. But when Dad dove into the vodka, she left. Well, they stayed married, but she was never home. There was always an art show, an exhibition, a gallery opening and so on. So I stayed up in my room while Dad went down to the pub to finish his mission of ridding the world of Guinness and Absolut, and Mum lived her life looking at paintings and sculptures. Still does."

I didn't know what to say. "I'm so sorry," I said, well aware of how pathetic it sounded.

"With the beer, he was fun. With the booze, he was, well, not so fun."

"Oh," I said, raising the level of patheticness.

"Yeah." Charlie bit her lip, not saying a word for a long time. "I never knew which version of him to expect. Not at first. After a while, I learned the pattern. When money was short, he'd buy a bottle of vodka. Did the job quicker, I guess. Not sure if he actually went to the pub those nights. More likely he went down to the river, under the bridge where all the alkies sat."

She shook her head slowly, snorting out a burst of tiny laughter.

"The other alkies, I should say. Every other month or so, he'd get some payout from the publishers. Royalties for the first two books. In the beginning, I think it was quite a decent amount. Then he'd be the centre of attention at the pub, buying round after round for his friends. Great friends that never would've said hello if they passed him by the river, though. Those nights he'd come home with dinner and cake from the pub. 'Come here, Lotty. It's party time!'"

A tear formed in the corner of her eye, fought its way over the brim and drew a tiny, wet line down her cheek.

"I loved him all the time, Ru. He was fun, and we'd sit by the telly, eating stew and cake and laughing at the screen. I loved him the other nights, too. It was just that he became this other man. A monster."

My own dad was my hero, just like Charlie's was to her. But mine had never been anything short of the greatest dad ever to me. I understood it had to be awful growing up with such a deadbeat father, and couldn't grasp how she could say she still loved him. The abandonment part, though, hit me right in the feels. Then again, what was worse—losing your dad to an unexpected death or watching him turn into a monster?

I walked to the sofa and sat beside her, taking one of her hands in mine. I just wanted to comfort her and didn't really think it through.

As it had done weeks before, a spark lit up in my mind. I gasped, feeling my own thoughts intertwine with Charlie's. A voice boomed. 'Look at the mess, you little shit. Is this how you thank me for throwing you a party, Lotty?'

A burning sensation on my cheek followed as the image became clearer. A man—the same man I'd seen in Charlie's memories that morning in September. Charlie's dad. He stood over a small version of my best friend. Her hand was on her cheek, but her eyes—oh, those beautiful eyes, were filled with fear and shock.

'You think I want to hit you? It's the only way you can learn how to behave.'

I desperately tried to get out of her mind, but her memories had glued themselves to me. There was nothing I could do but watch as her father hit her again. And again. Charlie—no more than ten years old —held her hands up in defence, but there was nothing she could do to fend off the oncoming fists. Finally, he stopped. My cheeks burned hotter than the fireballs I was able to produce, my heart pounding.

"Ruby? Ruby!"

I opened my eyes, not realizing I had closed them. Charlie was holding my shoulders, shaking me.

"Come back to me, Ru," she said. "Don't go in there. It really isn't a nice place to be."

"I forgot I could do that." I gasped for air.

She sat back in her corner, tightening her lips. Was she snickering?

"What?"

"You're hopeless," she moaned. "You forgot you

could read people's memories? What, you've got so many powers that you don't remember them all?"

I let my shoulders drop, and rolled my eyes at her. "Yeah, that's exactly how this thing works."

It was a relief. For both of us. The laughter seemed to wash away the painful memories, if only for a short while.

"I'm used to it," Charlie said. "It doesn't bother me that much anymore. I'm living proof that therapy is a great idea. It works. With Donna, anyway."

"That's good to know. I guess time helps, too." I had never felt the need for therapy, but the big, open scar in my heart hadn't healed in the seven years since Dad died. Not one bit. What could a therapist possibly have to fill it with?

"He's better now," she said, "I'll give him that. Drinks way less and has actually finished a novel. A draft, anyway."

"Is your mum still working?"

"Not quite as much as she used to. They're trying to patch their marriage together, but it's flaky. She keeps threatening to move back to Brazil. Though, as you say, time may help."

"Crossing my fingers."

"So you see, being alone is not what I do best," she said. "Let me rephrase that. Being left alone, that is. I'm fine on my own, don't get me wrong. As long as it's my own choice, you know?"

"I get it. And I'll never leave you behind like that again. We'll decide together from now on."

She put her fist out, and I bumped it with mine. "Deal."

"Besides," I said, "you're way too smart. And I need your magic."

"I agree with the first. I am wicked smart." She said the last part in what I assumed was a *Good Will Hunting*-accent. I wasn't about to tell her how bad it was.

"That's why I need your help. If you want to, that is."

"Doing what?"

"Paddock suspects some of his colleagues might be in cohorts with Harvesters. He says there's been a lot of cases lately where the police have used excessive force, particularly towards Mags. Several Mags have disappeared, if the coppers haven't killed them, that is. He's going to share his findings with me—with us, I mean. Problem is, I'm not very good at digital research. I know how to do basic searches, but I don't think that'll do the trick here."

"You're right about that," Charlie said. "The usual search engines are great for finding the latest Pinterest on cake decoration. For this type of digging, I've got my own magic. I didn't spend all that time alone in my room with my laptop and this huge brain for nothing."

Her grin was as broad as it was beautiful. My Charlie was back!

"So, think you can do some digimagic?" I asked.

"Hmm. If I hadn't known better, that might sound a bit condescending. But screw that, I like it. Digimagic. Maybe that'll be the name of my company."

"I'll be your first customer."

"Honestly, babe, you couldn't afford me. I'll be working big defence contracts and super-secret MI6 cyber spying."

"But before that," I said, "think you could wave your wand on this case? Also, Teagan, Brendan's sister, has a problem that we should look into."

"She's here? I thought she had run off with some douche."

"Yep. Her douche boyfriend is missing. She says he's been taken by Harvesters, somewhere north. I might get more info on that."

"Give it to me when you get it, and I'll see what I can find."

"That would be awesome. Whatever you can find on Goo—or wherever. Where do you search for stuff, by the way?"

She tutted. "Now we're moving too close to Digimagic's secrets."

I was about to raise my hands in surrender when my phone buzzed in my pocket. Not my regular phone, but the flip phone Paddock had given me. I picked it up and mouthed "Paddock" to Charlie.

"Hello?" I replied, for some reason thinking I shouldn't say my name. Maybe I was inspired by Charlie's mention of MI6.

"Miss Morgan?"

"Yes," I said, hoping my sigh didn't make it through to him.

"Care to bring your shifty friend for a stakeout this

Friday? Fernsby and his new partner are on the night shift patrol, and I thought we might get lucky."

Get lucky? I wanted to ask but thought better of it. "Sure, when and where?"

"I'll pick you up at—'ang on."

I heard him rustling some papers in the background.

"Nah, better you come to me. I'll text you later when I know which area they're covering."

"Great. What should we bring? Or wear?"

"The usual gear, really. Knives, shotguns—preferably sawed off if you have them."

I gawked at the phone.

"Just having a laugh, sorry. Normal clothes, but maybe ditch the high heels and skirts. And not too flashy on the colour charts."

"So black, then."

He chuckled. "Basically. Ok, talk to you later."

I put the phone on the table and looked at Charlie. "Looks like shit's getting real."

"What did he say? And when did you become all street and foul-mouthed?"

"Sorry. I can't help it, but it's actually a bit exciting. I know it shouldn't be, but—"

"Hey, I get it, Ru. And maybe that's a good sensation to bring into it."

"Maybe. Anyway, he wants us to join him on a stakeout Friday night. Hopefully, we can get some info on the bad coppers."

"Us."

I drew a breath, but before I said anything, Charlie

waved me off.

"Relax. We've put it behind us. Us means you and Jen on this occasion."

"No, it doesn't. Maybe me and Jen with Paddock on the scene, but we're depending on you as well."

"The digimagician, yes. And as I said, it's cool. I'll just do my thing back home, where my skills are best put to use. Go find Jen and fill her in. I've got some digging to do. Oh, and maybe start on a couple of the assignments in Canvas if I feel like it."

I gave her a quick kiss on the cheek and stood to leave. "I love you, Charlie."

"Of course you do," she said, slapping me on the thigh as I left.

Just before I closed the door to my room, she shouted, "And I love you, too."

I sent a text to Jen, asking her to call me. She hadn't come home after classes yet, and I recalled her saying something about a photo session in the afternoon.

Still feeling sad about what I saw in Charlie's memories, I sat on my bed, thinking about my own dad. As always, the mere thought of him brought back that big lump in my throat. I missed him so much and desperately wanted to get to the bottom of his death. I dropped back on my bed and lay staring up at the ceiling for a while. If only Dad hadn't touched the damned drug. I wished he had been a Mag himself.

Sometimes when I was a kid, I would lay awake at night, fantasizing about what powers I wanted Dad to have. At the time, flying was always my number one choice, most likely because I dreamed of flying myself after hearing bedtime stories of Faes flying in Avalon. Invisibility also sounded great, but Mum told me it wasn't a power any Mags had.

Was it that simple? Did he feel less of a man because he didn't have any powers, living with two Fae? It wasn't right, though. He never said anything other than how much he loved us, and he always treated me like a normal girl. That's how they wanted to raise me. They always let me know I was special, and that my powers should be used to help others. But they also wanted to protect me.

The past months had underlined what a dangerous world this was for us Magicals, but also erased any remnants of my feeling normal.

The words of Professor Kaine—I had to get used to calling him Gabriel—echoed in my head. If he was right, I didn't 'get' new powers. I'd had them all my life. Then why hadn't I known or felt them before now? The healing and force fields had been with me since I could remember. Mum told me I had thrown a field as early as two years old.

But reading—or seeing—memories? Fireballs? And the visions, if those were a power at all. I wasn't totally convinced. They had felt so real, though. But so far, I'd had no indication whether I had seen actual events in them. That could be another side of the memory reading thing, as it happened inside my head, I thought.

Gabriel was going to teach me to control my powers, and I looked forward to that. Both because it would come in handy if something happened, like on

Friday's stakeout, but also because I wanted to know more about my abilities. Were there more, for instance? Would I suddenly sprout wings or turn into a green giant?

I conjured two small force fields in my hands, shaping them and floating them at will. I'd never really checked how many I could control at the same time. Maybe this could be a training exercise? I made a mental note of asking Gabriel.

With the two balls hovering before me, I made three more, focusing on getting them the same size and shape. They looked like soap bubbles. Total control. I could send them slowly towards the window, stop them, and have them float back. I made them spin in a circle. Maybe I should try something a bit more challenging?

I didn't want to risk too much, though, so I made three of the bulbs disappear, holding the last two in my left hand. They were about the size of tennis balls, reflecting the light on the thin glass-like surface.

In my chest, I let the heat rise, feeling the surge of my fiery magic flow through my veins and nerves. Maintaining the force fields at the same time meant I had to divide my focus. A tiny, red hot ball formed in my right hand, no bigger than the marbles I used to play with when I was a kid. I tried to make the fireball bigger, but it didn't respond.

With a "pop" one of the force fields vanished. I bit my teeth together and made the remaining globe float towards the fireball. Gently, slowly, like a doctor about to perform open-heart surgery, I let the fireball rise through the air towards the force field. When they met right in front of me, the force field seemed to suck the fireball inside, enclosing its protective layer around it.

"Holy Lady Nimue," I blurted. "I did it!"

With a final push of my mind, I forced the translucent ball to shrink. As it grew smaller, the red of the fireball turned pink at first, then lighter and lighter until it was completely white. I wasn't sure if that meant it was hotter or colder, but never had the chance to find out. The force field had shrunk so much that it swallowed the remains of the fireball.

And vanished.

# NINE

Arms linked together as if nothing had ever been wrong between us, Charlie and I stepped inside Brady's on Friday morning, two days after we made up. The smell of coffee and bacon was thick in the air, and my mouth watered. But we weren't here for the food, although it would be rude not to order anything, so we walked up to the counter.

"Hey, Brady," I called.

The middle-aged man who had given the café its name skipped from one foot to the other, defying gravity as he turned a pancake in the air. Brady was as wide as he was tall and made a mean pancake. He sat the pan down and turned to us. A well-trimmed beard framed his broad smile, the light catching the sprays of silver between the otherwise ginger colours on his curly head of hair.

"G'day, Ruby. What shall it be this fine morrow? `Ang on!" He winked at me. "You fancy a cup of green tea with a squeeze of lemon, eh?"

I had struggled with placing Brady's accent at first, until he told me some of his life story one morning I was down here alone with my laptop and a half-written Whisper article. The gentle giant from Ireland had followed his heart, at that time attached to 'a sheila' from a little town way up north in New Zealand. His heart was eventually broken, but he kept the Kiwi slang, even though he had only lived there three years.

I smiled at him. "As every day."

"And for Señorita Charlie, one coffee, black."

Charlie grinned. "You know me too well, Brady. We won't be eating today, but I promise we'll swing by for some of your delish pancakes soon. I hope you stocked up on blueberry jam!"

"Aye, so I did. You and that lovely gal Jen ate all I had left. Where'd ya hide her t'day?"

"She's out shopping in central." I laughed. It was the truth. She had run out of the flat while shouting something about not having the right outfit for tonight. What I would be wearing was the least of my concerns, but to Jen, any occasion was an opportunity for a fashion statement. Even a stakeout.

Cups in hand, we turned to find Brendan and Teagan sitting in the far corner. I grabbed a seat next to Brendan, and Charlie sat down between Teagan and me.

"Hey, stranger," I said, taking Brendan's hand under the table. He gave it a light squeeze and offered me a gentle smile.

"Milady," he murmured.

Charlie cleared her throat. "Hey, I'm here, too."

"Hi, Charlie," Brendan muttered, though his eyes were firmly locked on mine.

Teagan took Brendan's other arm, yanking him closer to her, and his hand slipped from my fingers. "Does this mean she knows, too?" She pointed a finger at Charlie. "B, I thought you said we could trust your—whatever she is."

Charlie took a sip of her coffee, then placed the cup decisively back on the table. "As I said, I'm here. Brendan gave Ruby permission to tell me, and honestly, I'm your best bet. You won't find a better bloodhound this side of Cheshire. So to speak."

"Are you a Mag?" Teagan asked, catching me off guard. It looked like Brendan had a similar reaction. His entire posture changed, and his attention had moved entirely onto Charlie at this point.

"Does it matter?" Charlie retorted. "If you must know, I'm a hundred per cent human."

"Then what good are you?" Teagan sighed heavily, rolling her eyes.

It dawned on me that she might look like her brother, but her personality was nothing like his. If it wasn't for Brendan, I wasn't sure I would want to help her. Then again, there was a Mag out there who might be in serious trouble. No matter what he had done, I knew better than to want him condemned into the hands of Harvesters.

"Charlie is the smartest, most capable person I know," I said.

Charlie smirked. "She's not wrong, though I don't have any real magic. What I do have is super skills with computers, as well as a near-photographic memory. If anyone can find your man, it's me."

We were both tooting her horn a bit much. After everything, though, she deserved her time in the spotlight. "So, show me what you've got. Ruby told me she got a bunch of notes, but no picture. I could really use some visuals of Oliver."

Teagan sighed again. "All right."

She held her phone up, showing us the screen. A young man in his early twenties, with Hollywood-stubbled cheeks and a flashing grin, covered the lock screen as the background image.

"Cute," Charlie muttered. "Unlock it so I can send it to myself."

Teagan pressed her thumb down and gave the phone to Charlie to sort out the rest.

I leaned towards her and stared at the pictures as Charlie scrolled through the seemingly endless list of images of Teagan's boyfriend. His green eyes pulled me in, and my head started throbbing. My vision blurred as Brady's Breakfast flickered and began to disappear. A burst of light flashed before my eyes before everything went pitch black.

Turning my gaze to find a narrow slit of light, I squinted through the opening. I yelped inaudibly as someone pushed in front of me as if I was nothing but air. My body shook, and my head crashed into the low ceiling. I knew it happened, but I felt no pain. Whoever was in here with me had done the same, and he or she had hit their head hard. Not really sure how I could, I moved in front of whoever it was, then peered back out through the slit.

A row of trees rushed by on either side of a road. I had to be inside a car. No, in the boot. There were sounds of tyres on gravel, accompanied by the engine of whatever car this was as we took a turn up a narrow side road. There was a sign by the edge of the road. What did that say? I only had time to catch the last three letters before the person in the boot with me moved straight through me again. I crawled back on my elbows and watched him intently, attempting to adjust my eyes to the darkness.

The car came to a halt. The doors opened and shut, and footsteps followed. Light flooded the boot as the lid was opened, and the person beside me kicked both his feet into the air. They were shackled, and so were his arms. His head thrust back as someone slammed their fist in his face. I looked down as the man in the boot curled up; his face was bloodied and pale, almost unrecognisable. But I knew who he was. I caught a glimpse of a farmhouse and a peculiar weathervane before everything began to flicker again. Oliver's face faded, and my head spun. Everything shifted and disappeared, making me shut my eyes hard.

I forced my eyes open again. Brady's gentle face looked down on me, and something cold was lifted from my forehead. "There ya are," he said. "I'll just go get ya 'nother pack of ice."

Brady walked off, and Brendan took his place. "Are you ok?"

I blinked several times before I pushed myself to a sitting position, not without effort.

"I think so." I glanced at Charlie. Her eyes were wide, her mouth silently spelling out a question: "Magic?"

I gave her a quick nod, and she relaxed her shoulders, though I could have sworn she was suppressing a smile.

"You scared me," Brendan said, pulling me into his arms.

I inhaled the spicy scent of his Hugo Boss deodorant and sighed against him.

"I thought you were having some kind of seizure," he said.

"Sexy, huh?" I muttered, burying my head in his neck. "What happened?"

"You started shaking like crazy, then you sort of crashed onto the floor where you looked like you were having a fit, to be perfectly honest. Your eyes rolled back—"

"Definitely sexy then."

He breathed into my hair and chortled, hugging me tightly. "Definitely."

I reluctantly pulled away from him, suddenly conscious of where we were, and that a flock of random students were looking at us. Brendan helped me to my feet, and we found the table again.

Moments later, Brady returned with an ice pack and a glass of water. "Take care, now." He placed his warm hand briefly on my shoulder, then walked back to his kitchen.

"Well." Teagan pursed her lips. "If Miss Drama over there is quite all right, could we get back to finding Oliver?"

"T," Brendan said. "Be nice."

I waved my hands at them and found my chair again. "It's fine. I'm better now. Must have forgotten to drink enough water after my run this morning."

We had to find Oliver. He was definitely in trouble, but with the present company, I couldn't say anything about having a vision. I had no idea if what I had seen was past, present or future, but it had definitely been Oliver in that boot with me.

"So, where were we?" I said.

"I'm going to need his phone number, full name and any data on him," Charlie said.

"I sent all of that to Ruby," Teagan replied. "She can give it to you."

Charlie frowned. "Does she look like she's in a state to do anything right now? Just write it down here." She handed Teagan her phone.

It took Teagan a few seconds to comply, then another minute or so to type in the details. "There. You have all you need now?"

"I've already copied a few of the pictures of him, so yeah, that should be enough." Charlie accepted the phone back.

"I'd like to leave now." Teagan pulled at Brendan's sleeve. Her eyes were suddenly doe-like and innocent-looking.

"But Ru—"

"I said I'm fine, didn't I?" I put on my best imitation

of a smile. "It's all right. You go with Teagan, and we can hang some other time."

"You sure?" Brendan shook his arm away from his sister and scooted his chair closer to mine. His lips touched my earlobe as he whispered, "I happen to think you're the sexiest girl around. If there weren't so many people looking, I would have liked to kiss you now."

My toes curled, and I almost turned my head to meet his lips with mine. Instead, I leaned into him and whispered back. "Another time then, milord."

Teagan was already on her feet, her hands on her hips. Brendan excused himself, and the two of them walked away.

"Boy, am I glad to see them leave," Charlie breathed. "Not so much him, but his sister is one giant ball of issues."

I didn't say anything to that, but I didn't disagree either. "We need to talk, but not here."

We cleared the table and carried everything into the kitchen, where I left the ice pack and thanked Brady. Afterwards, we rushed out of the café and back to Craydon, where we made ourselves comfortable in Charlie's room.

"Shoot!" Charlie pushed back on her bed and folded her arms over a pillow.

No time like the present. "I had another vision. I'm positive that's what it was."

"Bananas! I can't believe you have another power. What did you see?"

Taking a deep breath, I shifted closer to her and

told her everything I had seen, including how the vision had felt, the letters on the sign and the strange-looking weathervane.

Charlie turned to her stomach, her elbows resting on the pillow. "The letters could be almost any word. I mean, how many places in England do you know that end in 'lds', right? But that weathervane, though, that might be our best clue."

"It looked more like a pheasant than a rooster. Hard to explain. I can try to draw it."

"Yes. Do that, and I'll see if I can locate where Oliver's phone was last online."

Could she do that? I was such a digital airhead. "How?"

"Easy peasy. I'll just do a trace on it. With all the information I've got, no problemo."

While Charlie worked her digimagic, I retrieved a pencil and a sheet of paper from one of her drawers and tried to replicate the weathervane I had seen. I discarded the first attempt, and the second one. On the third try, however, I got it right. At least enough so that it was recognisable to anyone who might have seen it, too.

"Ladies!" Jen's voice rang down the hall. She stuck her head inside and flashed us a grin. The sound of paper bags issued as she strolled into the room. "Aunt Jen brings presents!"

"What did you get?" Charlie eyed the bags eagerly.

"Only the perfect outfits for a stakeout. We're going to match, Ruby Ru." She stuffed her arm into one of the bags and pulled out a black pair of some sort of hunting trousers with multiple pockets on it, followed by a black t-shirt and a matching hoodie. Not remotely Jen-like. She cocked an eyebrow at me as if she had heard my thoughts. "It's designer made. Might look like nothing now, but you'll see, once you put it on."

"You'll look totally badass," Charlie said, her voice less bright than before. "Like Charlie's Angels." Her face lit up, and she gave herself a facepalm as the connection hit her. "That's it! You're my Angels, and I'm —well, I'll be home, not exactly looking as dope as you guys."

"No more sulking for you, young lady." Jen chucked another bag Charlie's way. "I got you something, too."

"You did?" Charlie's eyes lit up as she turned the bag on its head, the contents falling onto the pillow. I looked at it but had no way of knowing what it was.

"You'll be our remote eyes and ears. Our technical magician. With this, you can geek out, and look great doing it."

Charlie lifted the garment up and shook what appeared to be one single piece of black fabric with a red and yellow crest on it, a lion set proudly in the centre. She swung it around her shoulders, grinning from ear to ear.

"Where in seven ways to heaven did you get this?"

"I had it custom made. Figured you'd like it. I borrowed that old book you've been looking for, but you can have it back now."

"Jeannine Lune, you're my hero, you know that?"

Jen shrugged and sat on the windowsill.

"What is it?" I asked.

Charlie unfolded the garment and gave me a better view of the crest embroidered on it. "I think —" She squinted. "Jen, this is what I think it is?"

"As close as my guy could replicate it, anyway." Jen winked.

Frowning, I threw my hands up. "I still don't get it."

Charlie laughed. "This, my sweet summer child, is a wizard's cape."

"Ok. But—"

"It's from the book, silly. It doesn't really do anything, but it looks wicked cool."

Jen made a clicking sound with her tongue, then boxed her fist into the air. A shining piece of what looked like white gold was threaded over her fingers. A knuckle duster. Only Jen could make something like that look glamorous. "It's for you, Ruby."

"You're not wearing it?" I couldn't imagine walking around with a knuckle duster on my hand.

"I might have to shift, so no." She took the piece of metal off and tossed it at me. "I have one more thing, though. Another trinket coming your way, Charlie. It took some time to get it done, but the guy I ordered it from thought the project was so cool, he added an extra feature or two."

Jen flicked her arm out, and something spun towards the bed. Charlie caught whatever it was in one hand. It looked like a stick to me, though surely Jen wouldn't give Charlie a stick.

"You're fudging killing me here," Charlie squealed.

I shook my head in question.

"It's a wand, Ru! A super cool wand."

"You know wands aren't really a thing," I said.

Jen jumped off the windowsill and onto the bed with us. "This one is definitely a thing. Try the buttons, Charlie."

I narrowed my eyes at the supposed wand. There was one button at the bottom and another one on the handle itself.

"The one on the handle is for the flashlight," explained Jen.

Charlie pressed her thumb down, and the end of the wand lit up with a bright beam of light.

"This could come in handy." She swung the wand and said a few strange words that sounded like a spell of some kind, which was utterly ridiculous, of course.

"The bottom one opens a panel," Jen said. "But whatever you do, don't push the hidden buttons right now. There are three underneath the panel. Pink is pepper spray, blue is for a blade, and the black button —well, that's high voltage electricity. You know, in case you ever need to tase someone."

Charlie flung herself at Jen, her arms and legs wrapping around her like a child clinging to her mother. "Thank you, thank you, thank you!"

I stared at Jen. We had been so worried about Charlie, and short of placing her in a permanent force field, I'd had no clue how to protect her. This would give her an edge, and protection that would make both Jen and me relax a bit about Charlie's safety. It was genius.

An alarm went off, and I scrambled to shut off the reminder on my phone. "While I hate to break this up," I said, "we need to leave soon."

"Better get ready, then." Jen flashed her teeth at me in a feral grin. "Don't want to keep Paddock waiting."

Charlie planted her feet on the floor, flung the cape out behind her and waved her wand. "Your personal digiwitch, at your service. I'll hold the fort, and see if I can hack a few satellites."

# TEN

"See you, Angels," Charlie called as Jen and I snuck out of the flat. She had really adopted the Charlie's Angels' part. There was a light drizzle in the air, though not enough to get soaked. We pulled our hoods up regardless and bumped our fists together. Paddock had refused to pick us up at campus for fear of getting spotted, so we took the bus to Barnes Station where he would meet us in a civilian car.

We moved stealthily towards the Honda Civic parked on the side of the road, trying to act the part of badass vigilantes. More likely, we looked like a pair of idiots, but when in Barnes, and so on.

I tapped my finger on the windshield, and the window on the driver's side opened slowly. "Get in," Paddock whispered. "Ruby in the front, you in the back. Jeannine, wasn't it?"

"Jen is enough," she said, and we got into the car.

"You got enough room for your legs back there?" I

asked Jen, trying to move my seat forward in the tiny car.

"Just about," she replied. "I'll sit sideways, that works."

Paddock breathed heavily, rolled the window shut, and clasped both hands on the wheel. "There's food if you're hungry." He reached out and placed his finger on a switch, turning on the radio.

Static issued from the speakers. The radio, attached on top of the dashboard, was huge, with a range of buttons and lights. I knew absolutely squat about cars, but that radio was not a standard issue with the Honda.

"Where did you get this greased lightning, huh?" asked Jen.

Paddock twitched his nose but didn't turn. "It's my mum's."

I stifled a giggle. "Now what?" I asked.

"Fernsby is out on patrol with his new partner, Wes. We'll listen in, and follow them when something happens."

Jen stuck her head forwards between the seats. "How do you know something will go down?"

"It always does these days. London isn't exactly filled with only law-abiding citizens, either side of the fence." He glanced at the knuckle duster I was wearing, his brows furrowing. "You know how to punch?"

"Not really. Looks good though, right?" I waved my fist in the air.

"Not really." The corner of his mouth jerked upwards a fraction, and I was pretty sure he was mocking me, so I squirmed in the seat a little. The knuckle duster was no more than an accessory, and wouldn't do me much good. Besides, a fireball beat knuckle dusters any day. I shook my head at my own vanity and took the wannabe weapon off my fingers.

"If push comes to shove, I've got some other tricks up my sleeve."

"Try not to torch anything," Paddock said tightly, turning eyes front again, though there was nothing much to see outside.

We sat quietly and listened as time passed. I had imagined a stakeout to be more fun. Jen and I helped ourselves to the burgers and sodas Paddock had offered while we waited.

"So, there was this bloke." The sound of Paddock's voice in the silence made me jump, and I almost dropped the burger in my lap. "At the Academy," he continued. "He was top of the class in all the complicated investigating and legal subjects. Not so much in the physical aspects of the training."

I guessed Paddock himself was the opposite.

"I always figured he'd move up the ladder and one day become a hotshot in the Justice Department or something."

"Did he?" I asked.

"He's on the ladder, at least. Yeah, he's climbing it fast. At Scotland Yard. Met him at a seminar at a fancy hotel on Bayswater Road. Big deal with lots of high brass. We had a beer afterwards. Turns out he's in this task force at the Yard. Mag-related cases."

I stopped chewing.

The beams from a passing car flashed over his face

for a moment, highlighting the furrows on his forehead. "He was never one to break the rules at the Academy. See, when the rest of us went out drinking and messing about, he was always studying and preparing for an assignment or exam. We, and by that I mean especially yours truly, to be honest, always got in trouble. Once I stole—well, never mind that. Point is, whatever happened, Travers never said nothing. Kept his gob closed always. We became good friends, and I guess you could say we influenced each other. He helped me with the theoretical stuff, and I pushed him in PE. And we always had each other's backs."

"So, you're saying you trust him?"

"As with you two, I had no choice. But yeah, Travers is clean, and I do trust him. I—" He nodded at me and then back at Jen. "We can't do this alone. So, I sent Travers some info, and he took it to the Yard to look into it."

"What do Mag-related cases mean? For the task force, that is. Busting Mags?" I asked.

"Nah, they don't go after Mags in particular. They look for things that are out of the ordinary. A Mag stealing a watch at a jeweller's isn't going to raise their attention."

"But a gang of Mag-bashing coppers might?" Jen said from the back seat.

Paddock inhaled sharply. "Something like that, yes."

The silence returned as we all mulled over what this could mean. Time started slowing down again, and the monotony took over. When the burgers were gone, I attacked the chips. I was ten seconds from falling asleep when the radio crackled.

"This is Zulu Zero. Possible Ten-Ninety-One or Ten-One-Oh-Three at Chiswick skatepark," a female voice said. "It's old Mrs Claymore on the phone again. Probably nothing, but got to check it out regardless," the voice added.

"This is Zulu Two Zero responding," a gravelly voice replied. "We're two minutes out. Heading there now."

"That's them," Paddock hissed. "Fernsby!"

"Affirmative, Zulu Two Zero. Report on site."

"Affirmative. Zulu Two Zero out."

The engine roared, as much as a prehistoric Honda Civic could roar, when Paddock hit the gas.

"We're five minutes away, at least." Paddock grabbed the wheel. The tyres screeched surprisingly loud as he made a U-turn, speeding down the road towards Hammersmith, then onwards to Chiswick. Five minutes later on the dot, he turned off the headlights, and we pulled up slowly on the far side of the skatepark.

Jen rolled her window down a half-inch, sniffing the air. "Man, this place smells rank."

Paddock frowned, but his eyes were watching the skatepark, and so was I.

A police car had pulled into the park and two figures stood against it, having what looked like a heated discussion with three teenagers. The scene looked eerily familiar.

I gasped, the images of my vision from Monday

flooding back. My inner voice protested to the improbability of it all.

*It can't be!*

One of the figures was tall and lanky, while the other was a chunky, short man I recognized as Fernsby.

"Not good," Jen whispered.

"What?" I asked.

"They are asking the kids if they have any MagX on them. One of the boys says no, then—wait. 'No matter,' one of the officers just said. 'You're walking and talking bags of blood.'"

The car seat groaned as Paddock turned to look at Jen. "What is she doing?"

"Shush." Jen held a finger to her mouth. "He—I think it's Fernsby—says the kids can provide the blood someplace else. A farm?"

"Harvesters." The word slipped out, and I couldn't believe what I was saying, even with what Paddock had told us. It seemed so wrong for a pair of police officers to be harvesting on the side. "What else?"

"The kids are scared," Jen continued, her eyes wild. She closed them and her ears pricked up. "'Leave us alone. We've done nothing wrong. Don't touch her—'"

Fernsby grabbed one of the kids, a girl, by the arm. Something reminiscent of my force fields on steroids lit up between them, and Fernsby was hurled backwards. Was she a Fae too? The other kids jumped on their skateboards when the sound of a gunshot pierced the air.

Improbable or not, this was what I had seen in my vision. I had to stop what came next. I gripped the door handle as the girl fell down, and a sparkling blue light caught my eye across from her. The tall officer shoved a stun gun into the back of one of the boys as the third skated off as fast as he could, disappearing down the street.

"That's it!" I shoved the door open.

"Wait," Paddock said under his breath, but I refused to listen.

Instead, I ran, and I was pretty sure I could have broken all of my records with this sprint. Barely aware of Jen at my heels, I pushed on. The officers took turns, tasing the boy, his body convulsing at every jolt.

"Leave him alone!" I screamed as I closed in on the police car. My veins were on fire, my insides burning with rage. The sense of magic burst through me, ricocheting through my body, and I was not holding back. Not this time. I sped around the car, held my palms out, and sent a shiny force field to encase the boy, then hurled a second one at the girl, hoping I wasn't too late.

The officers stopped electrocuting the boy and screwed their heads towards me instead, both carrying a stun gun in one hand, and a regular gun in the other. My skin was crawling with flames as I formed a fireball in my hand while the force fields evaporated around the kids. I lifted my arm, staring at the raised gun in front of me.

A blur of white shot through my vision and the gun hit the ground as the wolf tore at the tall officer's arm. Blue sparks flew into Jen's fur, and she let out a feral growl, her teeth sinking into her attacker's other arm. The stun gun clattered to the concrete, and she continued to claw at the officer, though clearly with more effort than before.

I spun sideways, avoiding the electric charge aimed for my chest. Fernsby came at me from my right. He stumbled, but regained his footing and came at me again. I killed the fireball in my hand, afraid it might hurt Jen, before I tried to summon back a force field. My earlier switch to fire made me strain to make the magic work as I wanted, and Fernsby charged me again before I had a chance to act.

A second gunshot echoed in the night. I stared at the hole penetrating Fernsby's neck as he dropped to his knees and met the concrete, head first.

Paddock ran up to me, extending his hand while placing his gun back in its holster.

"You ok?" he asked.

"Never better." I glanced at the girl the tall officer had shot, then shifted my eyes to Jen. That officer would likely never regain breath either. "The kids!" I rushed over to the girl and placed two fingers to her neck. No pulse. The gunshot had gone straight through her heart.

"No, no, no!" I wheezed, my hand stroking the girl's hair. Maybe it wasn't too late? I had heard about people being dead for minutes, then suddenly sprang back to life. And though I was certain I didn't have the powers of a necromancer, if there was even such a Magical, perhaps there was still some life in her to save. With deep breaths, I gathered what strength I had left and reached for that calm, serene feeling, which was where my power to heal resided. A ray of scintillating light flooded over the girl's body. I held my breath and willed her to live. Gritting my teeth, I sent wave after wave of healing into her. There was no hint of movement, no sudden jerks.

I placed my hand flat on her heart and pushed with all my strength. "Come on!" Not a single, faint heartbeat to be found. A hand closed around my shoulder, and I stared up into Jen's sad eyes, my vision blurred by tears. She crouched next to me, stark naked.

"She's gone, babe. But the boy is still breathing."

I sniffled. Reluctantly, I left the girl's side, allowing the beams of light to linger in my palms. Kneeling next to the boy, I placed my hands over the scorched area of his exposed stomach. The raw sensation of magic sang in my veins as the shimmers of my healing power embraced him, his wound slowly closing, until it disappeared. The boy gasped for air, and I called the magic back inside.

"Thank you, Nimue," I whispered, offering a thought to the Lady of Avalon.

Paddock stood on the other side of the boy, looking at me. His brows dipped down at the edges and his posture sagged as if all the air had gone out of him. I glanced at Fernsby and the other fallen officer. No matter what they had done, this had to make Paddock feel awful.

He massaged his brow with his thumb and index finger. "You were never here. Go home."

"But—"

"I've already called the ambulance. They'll be here

any moment, and when they arrive, you and that wolf friend of yours need to be gone."

With shaky legs, I rose to my feet. "Thank you."

He gestured for me to go. "You did good. Don't worry, I'll clean up the mess."

The mess? Three people were dead, one of them looked like he had been hit by a train. It was a massacre to my eyes, not a mess. But we all dealt differently with grief, and Paddock had to be able to keep his cool when other police and emergency personnel arrived at the scene.

"Keep us posted, ok? And thanks again for—" I waved my hand at the scene.

"Don't mention it. Please. I'll be in touch." Paddock averted his gaze as Jen folded an arm over my shoulders. She was still naked, apart from the clothes she had wrapped up like a shoulder bag and flung over her shoulder.

"Let's run," she said. "I think we could both use it right about now."

She shifted back to a wolf. It was as disturbing to watch as it was awe-inspiring. It took her a few seconds, but the way her skin sprouted fur, and her joints cracked into different shapes looked painful enough.

I set off at a run, the Jen-wolf speeding steadily next to me. We detoured through as many side alleys and parks as possible to avoid anyone from spotting a wolf running through the streets of London. At the speed we were going, she could be mistaken for a large Samoyed dog or a crossbreed of some kind, but better to stay safe.

It was a long way back to campus, and I took the time to inhale the fresh air. The run doused the pain in my heart. I would not cry for the officers. The Magicals, however—them, us—made the tears gather in my eyes all over again. I let my feet carry me forward, the wind roll over my face and the light rain wash away my grief. If only for a short while.

Right now, it was just me, the ground below my feet, and the white wolf by my side.

# ELEVEN

MY LEGS PROTESTED WILDLY ALREADY, AND I HADN'T done more than walk a couple of hundred yards from our front door. Still, the best way to get the stiffness out of the muscles after last night's marathon through the streets was a light jog. I had thought of getting a bike, but I would never feel as free and safe in the city as I did back home on the gravel roads.

The air was crisp, and for once the fog was nowhere to be seen. If any Harvesters or shadows were out this early, I'd at least be able to spot them from afar. Not that I expected to see any of them, but last Saturday's encounter had me on permanent alert. One safety measure was that I wouldn't run the same route every morning. Maybe it would be smart to run at different times during the day, too, but I didn't want to give up these early hours.

The roads and paths through Hampton Court Park were mostly new to me. At barely six o'clock on a Saturday morning, the park was empty, at least along my route. I passed Hampton Court Palace and recalled seeing it in one of the Pirates of the Caribbean movies. Too bad Johnny Depp wasn't around now.

I decided to give my legs a break and turned back towards campus. A quick glance at my pulse watch told me I'd been out only twenty minutes. By the time I started the fight to get my hair dry after a shower, it still wouldn't be more than seven—maybe ten past. Good, that meant I could catch up on a little reading and maybe start plotting my photo story for the Whisper. It wasn't due for a while yet, but I had a shift at the cinema later, so whatever work I could put behind me would be a good investment, schedule-wise.

Thinking about the photo story, my mind recalled the images of last night. I was far from happy with leaving the scene, but Paddock was right. If we had stayed, Jen and I, we would have had no way of explaining our presence there. I only hoped Paddock managed to clean up the mess, as he had so elegantly—and rather morbidly—put it. The thought of it made my skin crawl.

As I passed through the campus gates, I almost turned and added a few more miles. My legs were fine and could easily manage. I loved to push myself on my runs, often adding a few interval sprints to get the extra cardio effect. Maybe I should do a couple of high-speed laps around the pond outside Craydon?

I leaned forward and was about to speed into a sprint when someone shouted my name behind me.

"Ruby!"

I skidded to a stop, almost losing my footing on the cobblestone path.

"Careful, child," said Professor Kaine.

I reminded myself of our naming agreement from last time we met. "Good morning, Gabriel."

"If it hadn't been for you standing here, bright and awake, I'd say it was an old man syndrome. But yes, I need my morning walk. Clears my mind. And what an absolutely splendid morning it is."

"Can't argue there. A bit nippy, perhaps, but I like that."

"Any plans, if I might ask?" The corner of his mouth twitched upward.

"Not really," I lied. I should do some work, but now I hoped he'd asked for a reason.

"Still interested in training, then?"

"Very," I said.

"Excellent. How about we go right now? Your workout will serve as a great warm-up."

On our way towards the old boiler room—my private magic gym—I told him about my vision of Oliver in the boot of the car.

"Parts of it seemed so real, like I was actually there. You know how dreams can feel very real, too. If you fall in a dream, you wake up with a jolt as if you were falling in real life. It was like that, only even more real. But then again, other parts were not like that at all. Blurry, if you know what I mean?"

"I do, and I've heard about this before. What you call visions, Ruby, has a different name in magic. True-sight. There aren't many magical beings with this power, at least not a very strong version of it. Real, pure Truesighters are among the rarest of all."

"Well, I'm not pure. Maybe that's why my visions— or are they called truesights, perhaps?"

"Both works, I suppose, but yes, truesights is the most common term."

"Right, so, as I'm only half-blood, that's why they are so blurry and fragmented, then?"

We had come to the closed-off building, and I lifted the police tape to let Gabriel pass underneath.

"I see bits and pieces clearly, and they are very clear. It's like I'm actually part of the scene. Then other parts of it are blurry. It's like watching unedited video clips. And some of them filmed through a veil."

The old doors creaked as Gabriel opened them, and the burnt smell crept into my nostrils. We climbed over ashen pieces of wood and debris from the explosion and soon found ourselves in the hallway leading to the boiler room.

We entered the boiler room, and Gabriel nodded at the torches on the walls. Without a second thought, I lit them.

"Impressive," he said.

I looked at my hands, quite impressed myself. "That was totally different from how it normally feels. I just —" I flicked my hand. "Like that."

"Your body is more in tune with your powers, Ruby. The exercise has got your heart rate and magical metabolism up and running. And to be honest with you, I wanted to see if I could catch you off guard. I think it's beginning to become part of your muscle memory. What most people don't think about, or perhaps even know, is that magic has a biological aspect to it. It's literally in your blood."

I looked at him, mesmerised.

"You see, it's all in you. As a Fae, even if you're only half—" He made a grimace as if he wanted to take it back. "It's actually not fair to use the word only for half-breed Magicals. They—you—are, after all, the second most powerful magical beings in the world. Pure-bloods are exactly that, pure Magicals with no human interference in their bloodlines all the way back when."

Back to Avalon. Growing up, Mum told me countless stories about our roots. Up until recently, I regarded most of it as fairy tales. Lately, however, I was beginning to think that the stories of another world might have more than a little truth to them.

Before I could say anything one way or the other about Avalon, Gabriel continued, "As soon as a Magical bred with a human or even a half-breed, the offspring could never be more than half magical. In fact, almost ninety-five per cent of all Magicals are less than one-fifth pure."

"And that relates to how powerful they are? We are, I mean."

"Magic is not an exact science, but as a rule of thumb, one could say that the purity level reflects the force of the individual's magic powers, yes. My point is that the vast majority of Magicals don't even know what they are. They never use their powers because they do not know they have them. The ones who do will usually only use a small fraction of their potential magic powers anyway."

"Because they can't control them," I said, starting to realise.

"Exactly! There is a common misunderstanding that Albert Einstein once said that humans only use about ten per cent of their brains. Although he never actually said that, it is a good metaphor for Magicals and their powers."

"So a Mag—sorry—a Magical with ten per cent magical blood can still have strong powers?"

"Stronger than they are aware of, yes. It has been commonly accepted in the science community that Magicals with less than five per cent magical blood—or to put it in haematological terms, those with less than fifty blue blood cells to each white—have no magical powers. Most of them live their lives thinking they are humans. This is positively false. I have personally witnessed a five-year-old boy levitate his pet dog. His mother screamed in horror at the sight. I had to calm her down, but all she kept repeating was that he's only four per cent. Luckily, no one else witnessed the event, so maybe she was able to keep it hidden."

I was spellbound by his words. With a pure Fae and a human for parents, I had never thought of my magic as powerful, not compared to Mum's. Still, the events of the past few months made it clear that what the professor said had at least an aura of truth to it. And it didn't go unnoticed in my brain how a mother was frightened by the prospect of her child being revealed. The little boy would probably be of no interest to

Harvesters with such low percentage blood, but a mother could never be too careful.

"With proper training, anyone can tap into their magical reserves and harness their full potential," Gabriel continued. "It all comes down to self-control."

If it was one thing I felt I lacked, looking back at how I'd used my powers since arriving in London, it was self-control.

"Tell me, Ruby. Is it hard to stop your powers, say the fireballs, when you're upset? Be it angry or sad, or even afraid."

"Absolutely," I replied. "There has been more than one occasion where I've had to retract an already lit fireball."

He raised his cane and pointed at a small pebble on the floor, about twenty feet from where we were standing. "You see that?"

"Yes."

"Pick it up and place it in my hand, would you?"

I started walking towards it but halted when he swung his cane in front of me.

"From here, Ruby."

"But I can't. I don't have any power like that. What's it called? Telekinesis?"

"That's one solution. But seeing as you don't have that, you'll need to use some other powers, won't you?"

I tilted my head at him, squinting a little as I tried to think of a way to solve the problem.

"Come on, child. This should be—" he began.

Like a stubborn, or rather provoked, child, I threw a force field down the corridor. It flew straight at the pebble, swooped it up like an eagle catching a fish on the surface of a lake, and returned towards us at high speed. Just as it was about to crash into Gabriel, I stopped it. It hovered in front of his face for a moment before I lowered it into his palm and retracted the force field, leaving the pebble in his hand.

What a rush! Charlie's words when she went flying over the water that night at Diane's party, high on MagX, were exactly those. What a rush. A knot formed in my stomach as I realised. I understood why she wanted to lick that MagX pane. Magic was awesome.

I looked at Gabriel, unable to contain my pride or my stupid grin.

"Excellent," he said.

"You didn't flinch," I told him.

"Why on earth would I flinch? Not in my wildest dreams did I expect you to hit me in the face with that thing." He dropped the pebble to the floor. "You see how easy it can be?" he said. "Want to try more?"

I was tired; the late-night marathon and this morning's run had taken its toll, and using both fire and force fields had drained even more of my energy. But I couldn't say no. Not now. This was far too much of an eye-opener.

"I do."

"Very well. How about we try it with your truesight, then? Let's see if we can tap into what you saw the other day. The sight with the boy in the boot of the car. What was his name?"

"Oliver." I closed my eyes and tried to clear my head

of everything else. Easier said than done, though, with all that rummaged around up there.

"That's right, Oliver," Kaine said. "Now come on, you can do this. It's all about concentration. Don't let any other thoughts clutter your inner movie theatre."

A tiny frame, like a polaroid, started to form in my head. Oliver's face looked at me from the picture. He was scared. I tried to grab a hold of the image, forcing it to turn into a movie, keeping the theatre theme.

"That's it," said Gabriel. "Go on, you'll get it."

He meant well, but instead of his words encouraging me, they irritated me. Disturbed me. He was pushing too hard. I put my index fingers on my temples, pressing against my skin. The image started to move, and Oliver faded out of the frame.

I opened my eyes, staring at the ground, then back up at Gabriel. I was gasping for air, my feet almost unable to keep me up.

"I can't do it." I swallowed the taste of failure. "I'm exhausted."

"Quickly, Ruby," Gabriel barked. "Grab the flames from the two torches furthest away."

"What?" The room was starting to wobble before my eyes. "I can't. I've got no more energy left in—"

"Do it! Now!"

I fixed my eyes on the torches, feeling my blood heat up. But instead of creating fire in my palms, I watched as the torches started shaking. The iron rings that held them to the wall tore out of the old bricks and fell to the ground, the torches following suit. I held out my right arm, fingers stretched, and grabbed the flames from both torches before they hit the dusty floor.

With the greatest feeling of control I had ever felt, I pulled the flames towards me and into my hand. As the last glare slipped under my skin, I lifted my gaze to Gabriel. His eyes were wide, reflecting the vanishing flame—they looked on fire themselves. And his smile. He looked like the grandfather any girl dreamed of. His white hair glimmered in the flicker of the remaining torches and—

"Ruby?"

I opened my eyes. What on earth had happened? Why was I lying on the floor?

Gabriel held my head in his hands, a worried look on his face. "There you are, my dear." He took to stroking my hair. "I'm afraid we went a bit too far. Are you all right?"

"I—I think so. What happened?"

"It seems your batteries went flat, so to speak. I do apologise for pushing you."

He helped me back on my feet, brushing the dust off the back of my windbreaker. My legs were spaghetti, but I managed to stay upright. It was as if I had just finished three marathons, back to back. I stared at the professor, his eyes gleaming.

"Sir," I said, forgetting our first name deal. "Are you crying?"

"If I am, it's because of you. That was the most beautiful display I have ever seen. You have immense powers, my dear Ruby. Immense."

I didn't know what to say. His words rang true,

though. And what I had just done proved it as well. This was far beyond what I had thought a Fae could do, let alone a half-blood like me.

"Did you plan that?" I asked.

"If not *plan*, per se, then at least I hoped it would work, yes," he said. "It was exactly the same as with the force field."

"So, by pushing me like that—" I started, the cogs in my brain slowly connecting.

Gabriel nodded eagerly as if he could see me reach the conclusion.

"You wanted me to fail," I continued, "to make me see that I was over-complicating things."

"So?" He dragged the word and rolled his hands to help me finish my epiphany.

"So, by trying too hard, I'm actually failing!"

"Voilà." He tipped his imaginary hat at me. "It's like a golfer. Not that I'm particularly versed in that sport, but as I understand there is a certain way of mastering the golf swing. Amateurs tend to want to swing as hard as possible to smash the ball down the fairway. A skilled professional, however, knows that it all comes down to control. They grip the club lighter, they swing with more rhythm and control, using inertia and physics to accelerate the golf club's head towards the ball."

Logan, my old editor—it felt like decades ago, although it was only a few months since I quit my internship—had taken the staff at Blacon Press to the local golf club. I never quite grasped the whole grip and swing concept, but the pro did say what Professor Kaine had just said, almost verbatim.

"So yes, not over-complicating is a good way of putting it," Gabriel continued. "And all I did now was use an old technique to help you simplify things. Back in the old days, before those German scientists proved magic to the world, people used to go and watch illusionists perform tricks at fairs and variety shows. They would pull rabbits out of large hats or make playing cards disappear. Some even sawed their female assistants in half."

I had read about those illusionists, as they were called. Their trade had gone downhill fast after magic proved to be a real part of the world. We learned about it in primary school. To me, it sounded strange not having magic around, as it had always been a part of my life. I guess it must have been quite a shock for humans back then.

"People were amazed, of course. The tricks themselves were not that hard and, usually, it all came down to sleight of hand. The important part, however, was the misdirection. Any successful magician had to be able to misdirect his audience's attention from what was really happening."

He pulled out a dark red handkerchief from his inside pocket. "Look at my hand." He raised the empty hand above his head.

I looked, of course.

"Now, where is the handkerchief?" Gabriel asked.

I turned my gaze down at the hand holding the piece of silk. It was empty.

"A simple party trick of olden days," said Gabriel. "Misdirection and sleight of hand." With a flourishing move, he made the handkerchief appear as if out of thin air.

"How did you do that?" I marvelled at him.

"The old illusionists, or magicians as they were also called, had a motto. A magician never reveals his secrets, so in honour of the poor sods, neither will I."

The word 'sod' sounded strange coming from him. I had seen examples of sleight of hand on TV, however. Some show celebrating the nostalgic times and trades, where one performer had done exactly what Gabriel had talked about. His skills, however, were nowhere near Gabriel's. I could swear that red piece of silk just appeared in his hand.

As he pocketed the handkerchief with one hand, he snapped his fingers with the other right in front of my face. "Quickly, what model was the car you saw Oliver in?"

"A Vauxhall Vectra," I replied instantly, seeing it clearly in my head. For a split second, I was back in Oliver's eyes again, observing what he saw when he was forced out of the boot. The letters were shiny and clear, except for the crooked L at the end of 'Vauxhall'. A gloved hand reached down and closed the lid.

"That's amazing," I said when the image vanished again.

"Well, yes and no. It's in you, Ruby. You are in control. All you need to do is take it."

My phone rang, throwing me out of the trance-like sensation. Jen's face filled the screen.

"Hi, Jen," I said, the words seeping like molasses from my mouth.

"Where are you? The girl is on the news."

That snapped me out of it. "I'm not far from home," I said. "Coming now."

I hung up and turned to Gabriel. "I've got to go, sorry."

"Not at all, child. This was a good session, don't you think?"

"Very." I gave him a hug, surprising us both, it seemed. "Thank you!"

He laughed. "Now that will keep an old man going for the rest of the day. Run along now, my dear."

# TWELVE

I BURST THROUGH THE DOOR, FLUNG MY NIKES OFF MY feet and ran into the living room. I hadn't expected Charlie to be up for hours yet, seeing as we had been up until two last night, telling her about the shooting. But there she was, next to Jen on the sofa, their eyes glued to the telly.

> "—example of how some of the Magicals misuse
> their powers. I'm not blaming all Magicals, of
> course, but this is an increasing problem and one we
> have to take very seriously."

The text underneath the uniformed policeman said he was 'Thaddeus Bolton, Chief Superintendent, Westminster PD'.

The image switched to a man outside an office building. He was sharply dressed in a white suit, his dark hair slicked back and sprinkled with silver. His brow was heavy over deep-set eyes, but his gaze was undeniably captivating.

*"First of all, our thoughts and prayers go to the family of the police officer. He is the last in a long line of heroes in the fight against the rogue Mags who seem to have started their final push."*

Jarl Colburn was every bit as charismatic as ever, and although he was being interviewed, he spoke as if he stood looking out at his congregation.

*"What do you mean by final push?"* asked the reporter.

*"Our church, the Children of Purity, has said this over and over for many years, Mindy: the Mags are not of this world. They aim to take over the Earth, forcing us humans out. I believe their war has begun."* He turned directly to the camera. *"When I am elected prime minister next August, I can assure you that my party, the Coalition of Purity, and I will introduce legislation to ensure the safety of mankind. Humans in the United Kingdom and the rest of the world will be safe from the tyranny of Satan's spawn."*

"He's a raving lunatic!" Jen snarled.

I had no words as I gawked at his bright green eyes that seemed to jump out of the TV screen. I shuddered, while the camera panned to the news reporter.

*"We will return with more on the tragic events of last night, where a police officer was shot and killed, and another died of gruesome injuries too horrifying to describe. The police suspect one or two Magicals, possibly Shifters. Back to you, Jacob."*

Jen muted the sound when the blonde news anchor switched to the ever-running Brexit chaos.

"Tragic, my arse," I said. "An innocent girl is in the morgue, probably next to that snake, and that's the real tragedy."

"I agree," Jen said. "But I think Paddock was right. At least I hope so."

I shrugged. "Tell that to the girl."

"I hope the boy you healed is ok," Jen said.

"Only one way to find out." I retrieved the burner phone from my pocket. There was only one number stored in the calling log. I hit the dial button.

"Have you seen the time?" said a very tired voice.

I couldn't care less. "How's the boy? The one the bastards didn't kill."

"I don't know, Ruby." Paddock yawned. "It really is way too early in the morning for me to know. He was taken to the ER, so I guess they have him under control."

"Who's looking after him?"

"The doctors, I presume. You know, those guys that work at a hosp—"

"I mean, who's protecting him at the hospital?" I snapped.

"Listen, Ruby, that's not how it works. I have no pull like that. He'll be fine, though. Take it easy."

If I had been a bull in front of a matador, I couldn't have been more provoked than by "take it easy".

Jen lay her arm on mine, shaking her head. "Don't," she whispered.

Holding my breath, I shook myself, then expelled the air slowly. "Fine," I ground out. "I just don't want him to get hurt. Or his friend to have died in vain."

"I get that," Paddock said. "And I want the same. But PSI Bolton has already concluded. Sure, there will be an internal investigation and all, but that's a charade. It will be ruled as self-defence, with the dead girl holding the smoking gun."

I stopped breathing again. So that's what cleaning up the mess meant.

"Before you go ballistic again," Paddock said, "there is nothing we can do about that now. The best thing to do is find whoever is behind it. Who's instigating all these coppers' raids against Mags. Travers is also in the loop."

"His task force?"

"Not yet," Paddock said, "but he's looking into the shooting to see if they should engage. We'll keep looking. Right now, we'll have to wait."

"I guess you're right," I conceded. "It's just not fair!"

"Again, I agree. Now, if you could let me catch a couple more hours' sleep?"

"Hang on a second," I said. "Could you check— after your beauty sleep, of course—and see if you can find anything about Mags being kidnapped?"

He hesitated for a few seconds. "Ok, I'll see what I can do."

"Great," I said, but he had already disconnected.

———

None of us could be bothered with any cooking, so we broke our previous record of how early we could order pizza. At twenty past eleven, Jen answered the door. Charlie sat on the sofa with her new wizard's cape flung over her shoulders. Jen put the two pizza boxes on the dining table, and I went to get plates and a carton of orange juice.

"I'll get fresh oranges next time, ok?" I said when Charlie came to the table and gave me a quizzical look.

"Hey, this works for me. It was you who said you wanted the jungle feeling."

For the first ten minutes, no one said anything. Any outsiders would probably have been appalled at how we devoured the food. I hadn't had time to think about it, but I was clearly famished. I could only imagine how Jen must have felt. Her animal metabolism meant she usually needed three times more food than Charlie and me.

"Good stuff," Jen said, gulping down half a glass of juice.

"You know," Charlie said, "if Mum had seen us, she would have freaked out. 'Two pizzas for only três senhoras?'"

Her impression of her mother made us laugh. Not that we had any idea if it was close to the original, but the Portuguese accent and the face she made was hilarious.

"Dos senhoras and one beast." Jen grabbed a big slice of the second pizza—the one with three extra helpings of beef.

"It's duas," Charlie said. "We're not Spanish. Anyway, I may have found something. On the coppers, I mean."

The mood changed in an instant.

"It seems most of—well, all of the major incidents lately with these extreme levels of brutality towards Mags, stem from the same area. Richmond, in the Westminster Police borough."

"All in the same station, then. That's not far from Richmond Park." If that wasn't suspicious, I didn't know what was.

"Yup. I did some digging into the officers. Some of them, at least. There are about five hundred at Richmond Station, so I didn't have time to check them all, of course. But I'm running a bot right now, scanning the various social media appearances of the names I was able to extract from the database. It was a bit scary hacking into the police, I must admit."

"But you loved it," Jen said.

"I defo did." Charlie grinned. "Not to make light of the tragedy last night, mind you. But yeah, it was a rush."

None of us blamed her. I, for one, was just happy she had stayed home.

"Ever seen *Goodfellas*?" Charlie asked. "The mob film with de Niro and Joe Pesci, and that other guy?"

"Doesn't ring a bell," I said.

"Dude, it's only the best mafia film ever." She rolled her eyes. "Apart from the Godfather films, of course."

"Of course."

"Anyway, the point is that de Niro is the leader of this gang. They steal millions. And then he orders all the members to lie low. Don't spend the money, as that will draw the attention of the cops, right?"

Jen pointed a finger at her. "But someone did."

"Someone most certainly did." Charlie nodded. "And de Niro had them whacked, of course."

"Really?" I grimaced. "Whacked?"

She rolled her eyes at me. "Yeah, yeah, keep up, will you?"

I raised my hands. "Go on."

"Seems a few of our uniformed friends have come into some serious money lately." She lay her phone on the table, turning it so Jen and I could see the screen. "Not exactly lying low, would you say? This is PC Malcolm Summers. And that's his 1995 Aston Martin Coupe."

Jen leaned closer. "It looks expensive."

"He bought it three weeks ago. Asking price was forty smackers." Charlie swiped to the next image. "And this goodfella is PC Ewan MacAllister. Now, it doesn't show in this picture, but less than three weeks ago, he made an eighty grand down payment on an apartment in Malaga. Not bad for a guy who has yet to turn twenty-six, and banks a salary of eight pounds short of twenty grand. And these are only two of nine I have found so far who match the pattern."

I whistled. "Too many to write it off as good economic planning."

Charlie pointed at the screen. "These guys are dirty rotten. Now, all we need to do is find out if there is a de Niro at Richmond Station."

The last slice of pizza disappeared from the box, and Jen held it in front of her mouth. "You make it sound a bit easier than I suspect it is." She shoved half of the slice into her mouth and bit into it.

"Hopefully I can find more. Just have to dig deeper." Charlie wiggled her eyebrows.

"Speaking of cars." I reached into my pocket. "I may have a lead on Oliver's kidnappers. Make and model of the car that took him. It's not much, but a tiny step closer, maybe?"

Charlie grabbed the note. "Where did you get this?"

"I watched a film," I said.

# THIRTEEN

On average, I clocked in about ten to twelve hours a week at the cinema, and mostly the work consisted of selling tickets, popcorn and soft drinks, and sweeping the gallery between showings. Tom, the manager, said I could work more if I wanted to, but although I could use the extra money, I had trouble enough already juggling school, the Whisper, and the cinema. And Brendan, luckily.

On quiet nights at the cinema, I'd usually be able to sneak in at least a couple of hours studying. This week, however, had drained my batteries, to use Professor Kaine's metaphor. Studies, the problems with Brendan —and they weren't any easier when I learned about Teagan and Oliver—and of course the stakeout on Friday night.

We were doing a special exam preparation feature in the Whisper for the weekend. I had three pieces in it, including an interview with a memory champion— apparently, that's an actual thing to be a champion of.

After our pizza feast yesterday, I spent a couple of hours working on the Whisper stuff before my shift at the cinema in the evening. Even though the turnout was low—the Russian drama on the screen could have had something to do with it—I was in no condition to sneak in my usual studying. I was barely able to keep my eyes open. When I came home from work at half past midnight, I collapsed on my bed without even considering taking my clothes off.

I killed the alarm and slept until 2.20 on Sunday afternoon. Charlie had made pancakes for breakfast—about five hours earlier, she made that abundantly clear—and I reheated three of them in the microwave. Charlie was in her room, fighting Gwen Stefani for the centre stage spot by the sound of it. I had asked if she wanted to join me for breakfast—or late lunch—but she was digging a hole in the dark web and wanted to see where it might lead her.

Three pancakes proved one too many. Miss wannabe-Stefani had been out shopping yesterday and blessed me with a large jug of orange juice, freshly squeezed from the actual fruits. This could be an issue, I thought, as there was no way I could return to the concentrated carton version after this.

I scrolled through the headlines of The Whisper on my phone. Raelynn had been to the O2 Arena last night, and titled her review: 'Madame X? More like Madame Ex'. In Raelynn's eyes, the old icon looked exactly the part of an old icon. Raelynn, or Rae as we all called her, had eased into the role of interim editor since Diane Cooper died so tragically. I shuddered from the memory of Diane's dead eyes staring up at me from the dusty floor in the old boiler room.

Rae was a good writer, no doubt about it. And although I didn't share her celebrity fixation, she knew how important such pieces were to attract readers. As had Diane. Clickbait pieces like the concert review Rae had posted also gave us something to show the advertisers when we needed more money.

It gave us the freedom to tell the truth that mattered, Diane had said. "I want our pieces to expose the misuse of power. Old school 'stick it to the man' articles." I hadn't known her very long, and I had even been jealous of her, and yet I found myself missing her. A lot.

I closed the browser and called Brendan instead.

"Ruby Ruby Morgan," he said brightly, elevating my mood five notches by the mere sound of his voice. "What can I do for milady today?"

"I just wanted to hear your voice," I said and meant every syllable. "I'm off to work in a little while. How's your day?"

"Just started, I'm a bit embarrassed to admit. I wish I could say it was because I spent half the night writing my term paper, but that would be a wee lie."

I laughed. "Why, Mr O'Callaghan, are you saying you went partying instead? Without your lady?"

"Without any ladies, in my defence," he said.

I could hear him stretching as he spoke and envisioned him on the sofa, legs on the table and with that glacier-melting smile of his while he talked to me. For a second, I wanted to end the call, ring Tom and tell him

I was sick, only to run over to Ealing to see Brendan. Was I really falling that hard?

"So, boys' night out, then. Sounds like you had fun."

"We did. It was nice to get away from the gloom around here." He whispered the last part. "I love Teagan to the moon and back, but I just needed to breathe for a few hours. She really paints the whole flat black and grey, Ru."

I half expected him to add "For missing a Mag", which of course he didn't.

"I wish I could tell you some news about Ollie," I said. "We're doing—well, Charlie's doing her best trying to find any clues as to where he might be." I desperately wanted to tell him about the Vauxhall and the weathervane, but then I'd have to explain how I knew about those details. The risk of him knowing about my Fae heritage was too high. And what good would it do at this point? He couldn't possibly do anything with the information—it was too fractioned and scarce. All I'd achieve by telling him about my powers was risk him dumping me. If I was close enough to his heart that he could dump me, that is.

"I'll let you guys know if we find anything useful," I said, hoping the nuance justified my lying. "I'd better get going, so I don't miss my bus."

"I wish you didn't have to work today," he said, underlining my yearning for him.

*Get a grip, girl!*

"Me too, Brendan. Me too."

Neither of us said anything for a few seconds. Or a minute. I couldn't tell.

"Still there?" he whispered.

"Still here."

"Hang up."

"No, you hang up." I bit my lip not to laugh. What a silly and absolutely wonderful cliché.

"Ok, we both hang up on three."

"Ok," I replied, well aware that I had no intention of hanging up on three.

"One. Two. Three."

Silence. I tried to up the volume. Was he breathing in the background? "B?"

"Ru?"

"This is way cheesy," I said, thoroughly enjoying it.

"I'll hang up first," he said. "That way, you don't have to, and I'll make you miss me."

"I already do. A lot."

"Run, milady, run for your carriage. I bid you farewell."

I looked at my screen. He had ended the call, and the clock showed me I was in trouble. Four minutes later, at half past five, I left the flat, not at all looking awake or ready for anything. The chat with Brendan, however, was worth it.

As I walked towards the large iron-wrought gates, I recalled the day I saw them for the first time. That Wednesday morning in September seemed ages ago, with all that had happened since then. A quick glance at my phone confirmed today was 1st of December, two and a half months later—and a lifetime of new experiences.

I looked up at the ornate letters at the top of the

gate. Scientia, amicitia et virtus. The first two words of the motto—knowledge and friendship—had so far come true for me, at least. Judging by what I had seen, with MagX dealers, Harvesters, and even a murderer, I had to leave judgment on the last one—virtue. Still, I had met virtuous people, so there was hope for this Fae yet.

As I stood at the bus stop, my phone chimed. A text from Charlie.

*Found a bit more on the coppers. Seems they have a secret society of sorts. 'Sentries of Camelot'. Very hush-hush, and buried in a chat room on 'Under-State'. Will dig some more into it, but I'm telling you—it's shady stuff. ttyl xx*

Shady stuff indeed. 'UnderState' was a forum on the dark web, a fact I only knew because Charlie had shown it to me when poor Ilyana went missing. My stomach churned at the memory of the police tent covering her body, which had been completely drained of all blood. Or exsanguinated, as I'd heard a student correct his friend when they walked away from the crime scene. Of all places to learn new words.

I read Charlie's text again. What in the world drove a group of police officers to run a secret society in an underground chat room? I wanted to alert Paddock but figured I'd give Charlie some time to find out more first.

I sent her a quick reply, with a shocked emoji.

*Great work! Keep digging, digiwitch.*

I finished it with the same two kisses she had sent me. The swooshing sound of the text flying towards her phone was replaced by the roar of the bus's engine a couple of blocks down the street.

I fished my Oyster card from the small pocket in the phone case. As I jumped onto the platform and swiped my card, I smiled at the driver.

"Quiet shift?" I asked.

"Lazy Sundays, love." She smiled. "I quite like them. Beats listening to my fella shouting at the rugby on the telly." She let out a laugh that turned into a coughing frenzy, bearing witness to a life of at least twenty a day.

"I bet it does." With a slight wave, I went to find a seat before she coughed up a lung.

There would normally be four or five other passengers, a couple of them regulars like me, but today there was only one. He sat on the seat behind the driver, the one I usually sat in myself. On any other day, the sight of a uniformed police officer would be reassuring, as it should be. Today, however, he gave me the chills. I had no reason to suspect him of being anything other than a decent, hard-working civil servant on his way to or from work, with every intention of protecting citizens. The recent events—and maybe even more, the text from Charlie—had definitely had their effect on me.

*You're really being silly, Ru!*

Annoyed at myself for thinking like that, I still decided to walk all the way to the back seats.

As the bus began pulling out of the lay-by, a loud hammering on the side was followed by "Wait up, please!" The driver hit the brakes and opened the door.

"Cheers, mate! Oh, sorry, ma'am! I forgot my bloody keys, would you believe?" Nick gave the driver a thankful pat on the shoulder and drew his hand across his forehead in relief. He swiped his card and sat by the window across from the policeman.

"Nick," I called.

He turned, smiled, and rose to come to join me.

"Where are you going?" I asked when he flopped down next to me. "You're not working tonight, are you?"

"I wasn't, but Tom called me and asked if I could step in. He had a bit of a bender last night." He wiggled his hand in front of his mouth.

The bus picked up speed again, and I recalled my first encounter with Nick. He had made a really bad first impression, and Jen especially despised him. He did set me up with this job, however, and throughout the few nights we had worked together, he had turned out to be much nicer than at our first encounter at the Old Willow.

"What do you want, tickets or popcorn?" he asked.

"You decide, either works for me."

"Let's flip." He held up a coin on the tips of his fingers. "Eagle says you're on tickets."

"Eagle?"

He showed me the coin. "American Silver Eagle. A dollar, basically. From last year's vacation."

He flicked the dollar in the air and caught it with his right hand before slapping it onto the back of his left. "Nah, you're pushing popcorn and Snickers bars tonight."

"Did you see the programme?" I said. "I'll be

shocked if we see ten people tonight. It was quiet yesterday, too, with that Russian film. I don't think I would have understood it if the director himself explained it. And tonight isn't any better."

"What, East German art films from the mid 70s? Tom has a weird taste."

"Almost. Hungarian. But I'll catch the one at seven myself, actually."

As we spoke, he rolled the coin back and forth over his knuckles. The large dollar seemed to float; it was quite impressive. I blinked when the coin disappeared, only to reappear the next second, together with two others. Nick manipulated the three metal discs with expert control.

"That's pretty cool," I said. "Where did you learn that?"

He swiftly closed his fist around the coins and put them in his pocket. "That's just a muscle memory exercise," he said. Did he blush? "My dad taught me when I was little. Keeps my tics in check."

"Oh, sorry. I didn't mean to pry."

"Hey, no problem. I wasn't even aware I did it. Ah, we're here."

He stood and took a small step back to let me out first.

---

The cinema wasn't one of the big multi-screen ones you'd find in central. The owners had specialised in niche films, although they had to include the major

Hollywood blockbusters every now and then to keep the wheels turning. This Sunday, the menu consisted of a rerun of an old 80s gem I had grown to love, *Betty Blue*, as well as the premiere of a Hungarian thing called *Love Hate Love*, running at 7 and 9.30 pm respectively.

I started watching *Betty Blue* together with about eight others but dozed off for the first time ever while at the cinema. When Zorg started fighting the orderlies at the hospital, I woke up with a loud "Huh?"

"Shush," said a girl three rows in front.

I waved a "sorry" and snuck out, almost cursing myself for falling asleep during that film. Had it been *Sex in the City: The Movie* I could accept it, but *Betty Blue*? I shook my head.

Nick sat behind the glass at the ticket counter, his hand keeping his head off the desk. I crossed the empty foyer and tapped the glass.

"Sold any tickets?" I asked my half-asleep colleague.

He stretched his arms above his head and let a jaw-breaking yawn finish completely before answering. "Nope. Guess a late night with some artsy-fartsy Hungarian flick has gone totally out of fashion."

The black and white monitor behind him showed the end credits for *Betty Blue*.

"I'll clean up in there." I nodded at the screening room. "It should take me all of thirty-eight seconds."

"We can probably close at half ten," Nick said. "If no one comes, that is."

"Suits me fine," I said and went to sweep the floors.

Ten minutes later, we stood by the kiosk counter,

looking at the black handles on the clock above the entrance. Two minutes left.

"What the hey," Nick said. "If we leave now, we'll catch the 9.37 back to campus. You in?"

"In a world where every rule was to be obeyed, they chose to break them all," I said, trying to lower my voice to film trailer levels.

"Students by day, outlaws by night," Nick replied, doing a much better impression than me.

He walked towards the ticket booth where the light switches were, while I leaned behind the sweet counter to grab my jacket.

A bright flash filled the foyer and blinded me completely. I rubbed my eyes, trying to get rid of the yellow dots. My vision slowly adjusted to the darkness, a small gleam of light coming through the glass entrance doors from the street.

"Holy shit," Nick shouted from the back room. "Must have blown the gaskets. You ok, Ruby?"

"I'm fine," I called. "We should probably call Tom, though."

A thud and a muted scream sounded through the dark foyer. Nick probably hit his knee on the chair.

"Nick?"

Silence.

I pulled my phone from my pocket and switched on the flashlight before moving towards the back room. "Nick? Don't mess around, please. It's not funny."

The idiot was bound to be hiding behind the door. I had no intention of letting him scare me, which was a total lie. Inside, my heart was pounding.

"Come on. We'll miss the bus!" I kicked the door wide open, expecting to hear an "Ouch" or something. Instead, the door slammed into the small safe behind it. The thin ray of light from my phone landed on Nick's slumped body.

"Nick!" I dropped to my knees beside him and grabbed his shoulder. "Are you ok?"

He didn't answer. His chest moved ever so slightly. Thank the Lady! He was still breathing. He must have tripped in the darkness and knocked himself out. Healing him would be easy, I figured, but I had to make sure I stopped the magic before he woke up. I didn't want him to know.

At first, I started to draw my breath as I usually did when I wanted to summon the healing power. Then I remembered my training with Professor Kaine. No need to make a big song and dance of it, I told myself. Just let it loose. I put my hand on Nick's chest and sent a warm flow of healing magic into his body. I kept an eye on his face, ready to let go the instant I spotted a reaction.

I yelped as something tightened over my chest, jerking me backwards. My hand slipped from Nick's still body. There hadn't been enough time to heal him. Instinctively, I tried to wiggle free, reaching for the rope squeezing the air from my lungs, but my arms were locked to my body. My heart raced in panic, as the realisation hit me. The Harvester from Richmond Park was back. I had avoided running in the park since, and he'd found me anyway.

My heels hit the threshold as my attacker dragged

me into the foyer. Inside me, the forces I had inherited from my ancestors stirred, and I let them surface as a force field in my palms. As I prepared to flick it back to encapsulate my attacker, a sting of pain shot through my neck, sending spasms of electricity through my body.

"No point, missy," said a raspy voice. "Ulfius, put it on. Quickly!"

There were two of them?

Anger replaced my fear, and I called upon my fire-power instead. A pair of hands locked around my neck, and I released all my energy in a single burst.

The hands let go, and the owner screamed like a wounded dog right next to my ear. "Zap that Maggot again. She's on fire!"

Bracing for another shock of electricity, I gasped for air as the pressure around my chest weakened.

"For fuck's sake," shouted the raspy voice again. "I lost my zapper. Hold her still!"

I spun around, swiping my legs along the floor like a breakdancer, and hit one of the attackers' legs with my shin. I cried out. The pain was excruciating, but I couldn't stop. I tried to get to my feet. A sort of crawling on all fours was all I could manage, however, and I had no idea where to go.

The rope that seconds before had been around my chest burned and coiled like a red and orange snake drawn from the floor to the outline of a man on his knees. Another man stood next to him, hunched over and shaking his hands—hands he had used to hold my neck when I pushed flames from my skin.

I scrambled to my feet and stumbled into the screening room, hoping the darkness could play to my advantage. Once I found my footing, I was able to move faster, limping down to the fourth or fifth row of seats. I threw myself in between them and dropped back on all fours.

The door swung open, crashing into the wall. Beams from two flashlights swerved from side to side. There was no way they wouldn't find me. I was a rabbit, stuck in a corner, and the foxes were coming.

I pulled my phone from my pocket, easing it up to my face. Shielding the screen with my hands, I tried to call Jen.

No signal!

I remembered the Facebook update from Tom last week, where he bragged about how he'd installed a mobile phone jammer in the cinema. Focus on the big screen, not the little ones, was his mantra. A mantra that might very well turn out to be my demise.

Pocketing my phone, I started to wiggle backwards. If I could only get to the door.

I yelped as my body cramped up; a paralyzing pain burned through me. Staring into the darkness, my body jolted between vigorous tremors and a numbing stiffness, blue sparks flashing before my eyes. After what felt like an eternity, the convulsions stopped.

"A feisty one, this one, eh, Ulfius?"

I tried to locate the direction the voice came from.

"I'll say," replied the other one.

Their voices were strange and metallic, near and far

at the same time. Like the audio from a black and white film in the forties.

Something locked around my neck. I tried to scream, to push at my magic. Nothing worked. The thing on my neck buzzed, sending a low, sizzling stream of electric current through my body.

"What about the bloke out there?" Ulfius asked.

"Bag 'im."

"Leave off, Lionel! He ain't never seen us."

"Shut up, Ulfius. Bag 'im, all right?"

"Fine," Ulfius said. "Look, she's still awake."

"Not for long," Lionel said.

Blue sparks flashed before my eyes, and then Lionel's words came true.

# FOURTEEN

Silence.

Darkness.

Darkness and silence.

My body jerked awake, my senses straining for control. A strong smell of chemicals crept into my nostrils, and I wrinkled my nose. My face hurt. I became vaguely aware that the rest of me hurt just as bad. But from what?

An attempt at shifting my weight ended in more pain, a wave of shock coursing through me, my limbs constrained by ... something. My mind slurred like the worst hangover as I tried to grasp a strand of coherent thought. A sudden movement sent me bouncing where I sat, my back screaming in agony. My eyes resisted violently to my attempt at opening them.

Sounds. My ears buzzed at first before the humming noise of an engine grew increasingly louder. My head hurt, too. Where in the darkest parts of Avalon was I?

"Ruby," someone whispered a million miles away.

I tried shaking my head, gasping as a shock of electricity closed around my neck.

"Ruby," the voice repeated, closer now. "Stay still or you'll hurt yourself more."

I opened and shut my mouth, unable to get words out.

*Focus, Ru. You can do this. Focus.*

Releasing all thoughts of pain and the weight of cold fear, I channelled my strength into opening my eyes. Slowly at first. Blinking. A haziness clouded my sight, and I blinked some more.

"There you are, Ruby."

"N-Nick?" I wheezed.

The room rattled, my eyes gradually adjusting to the dim light. Nick sat on a pulldown seat opposite me. His arms were behind his back, his feet bound.

"Who the hell were those guys?" he asked.

Guys? *Oh, crap.* Those guys! The fear ensnared me as everything came rushing back. No! Hell no! This was not happening. I stared at Nick. Even in the darkness of —what was this, a van? It had to be. Even in the darkness of the van, a bruise was clearly blossoming on his cheek. His usual cheerfulness was wiped from his features, and we were trapped.

This was happening.

"I don't know," I muttered.

He glared at me then. "I think maybe you do."

"Why, what makes you say that?" My voice was still hoarse, though it came out clearer this time.

"I don't know. Maybe because you're the one in

chains and a freaking Fort Knox collar around your neck, whereas whoever they are decided rope was good enough for me."

I grimaced. What was I going to tell him, other than the truth? We had been taken by Harvesters—no doubt in my mind—and one way or the other, he would realise what I was. If he hadn't already.

"Those guys," I stammered. "They're Harvesters. And they've been after me for a while, I think."

His eyes widened as he came to the conclusion on his own. It was one thing to think about what this said about me, however, and an entirely different thing to hear it directly from the Fae's mouth. I was going to have to tell it to him straight.

"As you may have already figured out, yes, I'm one of those, how did you say it?"

"Bloody freaks," he offered reluctantly.

"Yep, I'm one of those."

We sat there, staring at each other for a while. Eventually, Nick's gaze fell. "That was a mean thing to say. I know that. Jen has given me shit about it for weeks, and she's right. I've got a big mouth. I'm really sorry." He sucked on his lip for a moment. "But you have to admit, weird shit happens when Mags are involved. It's a ton of scary."

I could kind of understand where he was coming from. "All right, then. Any idea how to get out of here?"

"Me? You're the one with magic." He frowned. "You do have magic?"

I sighed, my head spinning again. "I'm also chained

up and served jolts of electricity whenever I move too much." This was not good. Not at all.

"Any idea who these Harvesters are? Where they're taking us?" he asked.

"No, I—" My mouth closed over the words. What did I know? I knew a few things. What had Charlie said in her text? Something about a secret group, Sentries of Camelot. "I think they're coppers. Of the corrupt kind."

"Bobbies? No way!"

I nodded, my body shaking involuntarily as the van made a turn, and I winced at the sudden shock of electricity shooting down my spine. The sound of wheels on gravel was unmistakable as the van slowed its pace. We had to get out.

I reached for fire. A sense of warmth settled in my gut like a small internal hearth. But nothing happened. Too tired, restrained and weak as I was, I couldn't reach the fire, couldn't summon it forth or catch my grip on it. I would have shaken my head, but I was afraid of what another jolt would do to me at this point, and I didn't want to pass out again.

*Well, Ruby Ru, you're sure hip-deep in it now,* I thought to myself.

"Well?" Nick asked.

"Nothing. My magic won't react. I'm spent."

I had always felt powerful. Even as a little girl, throwing my force fields around the garden, catching small butterflies only to release them again in a bed of flowers. It had always been easy, a part of who I was. Who I am. Since adding a few powers to my list of abilities, I had to admit—if only to myself—that I was enjoying the surges of power, the sense of almost being indestructible.

I bit down on my lip. Humans taking MagX had never made sense to me before. But maybe this was what it was like? Right now, I felt utterly powerless—human. I would have sold my soul for a bit of magic in that instant. The kind of power people died for.

Nick shook his head at me, and I could see my own fear reflected in his eyes. We were both aware of the obvious. We were utterly and royally screwed.

The van rocked as the driver hit the brakes. I tensed, expecting another shock, and exhaled carefully as none came.

"What the fuck took you so long?" a voice boomed outside.

"Bloody engine again. I told you we should get a new van."

"It's gone four in the morning," the first man said. "Right, let's get her out of there."

A spear of light shot into the van as the doors opened.

"Welcome to the Farm," a deep voice said.

A large man peered at me before his grey eyes settled on Nick. "Damn it, Ulfius. Who's the boy?"

A gangly man climbed inside. His hands were too big for his body, and he had the kind of face that could be mistaken for a thousand other faces, the kind you would never look twice at in passing. In this instance, however, I looked hard. Any detail might be significant, and I wanted to remember everything in case we did manage to wiggle ourselves out of this mess.

"Chill, Morien," the gangly man said. His voice was as forgettable as the rest of him.

"Mordred," the other man replied in a clipped tone. "Blimey, Ulfius. I'm Mordred, Pete is Morien." He glanced at me and slapped himself on the forehead.

Ulfius threw his hands up in an apology. "I get the damned names mixed up. Sorry, Mori—Mordred."

Mordred leaned his bulky arms on the doors, his brawny body blocking out most of the light beam. In the dim glow from the bulb inside the van, I could barely make out his features. His bald scalp was covered in scars, the tip of his nose bridged inward. Every part of him looked hard and tight.

"Who is the boy?" he said.

A third man came up behind Mordred. "A loose end."

I recognised the voice from the cinema. He was one of the men who had caught me. Ulfius, or whatever his real name was, had to be the other.

"Why is he not chained, Lionel?" Mordred snarled, spit forming at the edges of his mouth.

"He's not a Mag, sir." Ulfius brought some kind of weapon up in one hand while releasing Nick's ropes from the wall, then proceeded to drag Nick outside. It took me a moment to piece together what the weapon was. I had seen it before, at the skatepark. The kind of advanced stun gun the coppers had used on the kids.

The third man, Lionel, jumped into the van. His bald scalp glistened with sweat, and a few stubbles were visible above his ears. He probably shaved it all to conceal his receding hairline. Instead of working to his benefit, it accentuated his chipmunk cheeks and large potbelly. An enormous keychain dangled from his belt, the noise rattling in my ears. Unable to fight my fatigue, my eyes slid shut for a moment. Something clicked like a key in a lock before a pair of strong hands clasped around my arms, forcing me up and outside after Nick. The glare of the sun stung my eyes as I opened them again. My knees hit the dirt.

I shifted my gaze around. Lionel held onto the chains attached to me, but all three men were looking at Nick.

Mordred spat at the ground, then fished a pack of smokes from his pocket and lit a cigarette. "What do you propose I do with him?"

"I wanted to whack him, sir," Ulfius said.

Mordred slapped Ulfius over the back of his head, then leaned over Nick. "Maybe we should put you down."

Nick's eyes were wild with fear. I wanted to help him, torch the ground and the coppers with it. I looked around for an out. Anything that might give me an advantage. Where on earth were we?

Hay bales lay on the fields surrounding us. I counted two farmhouses, and one very large barn a short walk away on the top of a hill. Something was off, though. Something was missing. I narrowed my gaze, the wheels in my mind turning furiously to make sense of the place. The pieces clicked together, snapping into place. There were no animals. Not a single cow, sheep or pig. There wasn't even a rooster or a cat anywhere in sight. On the roof of the barn was a strange-looking weathervane. My eyes sprang wider. I had seen this place before.

Ulfius grabbed the rope tied to Nick's hands, tugging it hard. Nick made a disgruntled sound but said nothing. "Want us to shoot him out back behind the barn?"

*Oh, please, no!*

Mordred crossed his arms. He was large, like a contestant in a strongman competition. His stance was calculated, his frame proud. Everything about him screamed ex-military. If only I could reach my magic.

"No," he muttered. "No. This is not how we do things. Humans are not part of the deal here. We might have to kill him, but it won't be my call. I'll take this matter to Galahad. He's due for a visit tomorrow."

Galahad? I knew that name from somewhere. Wasn't that a knight?

*Sentries of Camelot, of course!*

They had taken their code names from Arthur's knights.

"Take the boy to the main house for now," Mordred ordered. "I don't want him inside the Farm."

Somehow, when Mordred said farm, I didn't think he meant it in the way people usually did.

Ulfius shrugged and walked off, dragging Nick with him. Bound as he was, he crashed to the ground like a load of bricks. Ulfius tugged at the rope, but Nick was bigger than him, athletic and strong.

"Need a hand there, Ulf?" Lionel offered, handing my chains over to Mordred before taking hold of the ropes with Ulfius. The two of them lugged Nick along up the hill. He cried out in pain this time, squirming and bouncing the whole way.

Their voices travelled as the sentries spoke between pants.

"Think she's a Pure?" Ulfius asked. "I haven't had a taste of that PureX yet."

"We'll see when we test her." Lionel's tone had a mischievous edge to it.

"If not, we might find a donor among our cattle somewhere. There have to be more Pures out there, and I really want a taste." Ulfius halted for a moment. "I hear it's like power central, like the sweetest nectar imaginable. And much more sustainable." He snickered, and his whole body vibrated, like a kid walking into a sweet shop.

My chest tightened, my breath catching in my throat as I watched them disappear. Pures. PureX?

A shadow fell over me, derailing my attention.

"Now, then, Ruby Morgan." Mordred's grey eyes focused entirely on me this time.

I flinched at the mention of my name. But of course he knew who I was, otherwise he wouldn't have kidnapped me.

I saw his face clearly now. The scars didn't just cover his scalp, they crisscrossed over his temples and cheeks, and cavernous furrows and evidence of a life that had once been spent somewhere much warmer than England showed on his skin. Deep-set brows and a broad chin completed his terrifying features.

"You're a hard fish to catch. I sent some of my best

officers after you, and you've slipped through their fingers more than once."

"Why am I here?" I asked. Stupid question, but what else did I have?

"We'll see. Once we've sorted out your status, we'll see."

"Status?" I said.

"We usually find our own fish. But you, you're here on high authority. Makes me wonder—"

I shivered. Why did someone want me specifically? Had I stuck my head out that far? If this place didn't kill me, then Mum would. Though her methods would undoubtedly be more merciful than these sorry excuses for Arthurian knights.

"Depending on our findings, we'll talk again." Mordred pushed me, forcing the air from my lungs.

My eyes closed once more, catapulting me back into darkness.

# FIFTEEN

MORE DARKNESS.

I coughed against the stale, dry air, then stopped, turning the cough into gently clearing my throat. I was not in the mood to get zapped again. I let out a steady breath of air when nothing happened. My joints ached, and the sound of screeching metal somewhere above tortured my ears.

I stretched my fingers. The shackles on my wrists were gone. Slowly, I raised my hands, carefully brushing my fingers over the cold, sleek collar still fastened around my neck. My eyes watered, tears threatening to spill out. Panic tore through me, and I wanted nothing more than to run. From wherever this place was. I blinked as the memories began flooding back.

Nick! Where was Nick? It took me a moment before I remembered the Camelot impersonators dragging him off to only the Lady knew where. He was human. A loose end, Lionel had said. And what did one typically do with loose ends? I shuddered, my heart rate rising. He was going to die. And the only reason he was even here was because of me. I couldn't help him. I couldn't even help myself, as it was. But I had to find a way out.

Muffled voices sounded somewhere in the distance as I peered out at the dimly lit room. The fields were gone, there were no hay bales, no trees. Instead, thick metal bars separated me from a room that looked nothing like any farm I'd ever been to. And I had been to a few farms before, seeing as how there were a lot of them in Cheshire. I had often spent my summers helping out with the horses on a nearby farm in Cheshire. Dad used to love watching me ride. That was years ago, however, and this was now.

My heart raced, looking for a way out. I gripped the bars in frustration, my body convulsing from yet another electrical shock, tremors bouncing through my bones, sending me into fits on the floor. Spit trickled from my mouth, and my eyes rolled back.

I had no idea how long I lay there afterwards. Exhaustion encased me, my fear turning raw and numb. If I could have healed myself, this was the time to do so. But I couldn't. I couldn't even reach a tiny spark of power, let alone produce any magic that would help. Not that I could heal myself at full strength either, but if I could only catch my breath and find some string of magic, and tap into the fire that was surely still some-where inside me, then perhaps I could melt the bars. I could burn this entire excuse for a farm into nothing but cinders. My fear took a backseat as a growing sense of anger twisted inside. I had to control my emotions, or I would never get out.

And then there was Nick.

With nothing else to do, my mind ventured into thoughts of revenge. The image of Mordred on fire actually produced a quirk of my lips before I caught myself. What was I thinking? I had to come up with a plan of escape, not worry about revenge. That wasn't me. Was it? I slid my hands into my pockets, searching for my phone. Empty, of course. The Camelot coppers might be cruel and possibly not among the brightest of the bunch, but of course they had the wits to take my phone.

My eyes shifted, and I turned my head sideways, not testing my ability to sit yet. A fluorescent light illuminated enough of the room to see shapes, and the amounts of steel and grey colours, which made up the colour-combination of the space. There was a partial second floor constructed of metal grates like some kind of mesh I'd seen in prison films. Two sets of staircases led up to it, maybe ten feet away from me.

Stifling a scream, I bit my teeth together, my lips tight as my emotions got the better of me, yet again. Cages dotted the floor above to the right. Lots and lots of cages. My stomach revolted, and bile threatened to rise in my throat. A couple of figures moved along the cages. A cage door opened, and a flash of blue light followed. A smaller figure shook and thumped to the floor, out of sight. I averted my gaze. There was nothing I could do. So I did the only thing I could do, kept looking at my surroundings. There were cages on my floor, too, though not as many as above.

There were metal tables like the ones I'd seen in crime series when the detective visits the morgue. A double metal door, at least twice the size of a normal double door fridge, faced me a couple of feet to my left. I shuddered in horror at the syringes, the multitude of blood bags, the vials, the panels, and a highly advanced array of chemistry equipment, all neatly arranged around the room. I turned away from the sight, the taste of bile now coating my tongue.

The image of the boiler room where we had found Jen hanging from the ceiling, tubes attached to drain her blood, forced itself into my mind. But the janitor and his accomplice had been sloppy, acting on their own. They were messy and unorganised, whereas this —this was something else entirely. This was calculated and refined in an eerie, screwed up kind of way.

I looked past the steel bars of my cage and through the bars of a neighbouring cage. If I stuck my arm out, I could probably have touched it, but that would undoubtedly mean blacking out again, and I was not about to do anything rash.

A pair of wary eyes stared back at me. I had no way of telling their colour in the dingy light, but I would guess a dark hazel. The girl couldn't be more than thirteen or fourteen. Her raven-black hair was straight, long, and knotted. She had a worn look on her face that did nothing to hide her smooth features, high set cheekbones and her broad button nose, which had recently been running with snot, that had dried above her upper lip. Streaks of tears painted her cheeks, creating thin patterns in the dirt covering her bronze-tinted skin. She met my gaze, a slight tremor on her lips.

"Hey there," I croaked, the sound coming out distorted and wrong.

She didn't reply, just looked at me with the kind of dread of someone who had stopped fighting and submitted to the terror of her doom.

"I'm Ruby," I said. "What's your name?"

The girl hugged herself tightly. "Kaede," she whispered.

"Cade. With a C?"

"No, with a K."

"Does it mean anything special?"

"It's Japanese," she said. "Means maple."

"What a beautiful name." I drew in a breath, attempting to steady my voice into a more amiable tone. "Nice to meet you, Kaede." I tried pushing myself up, only to stop the motion as soon as it began. I had to save energy. "Would you happen to know where we are?"

"They just call it the Farm. I don't know. I was in Bournemouth one day, the next I found myself in the boot of a car on my way here."

Nothing new then. I sighed, then backtracked. I was brought here in a van. Oliver and Kaede were both brought here in the boot of a Vauxhall—or at least that was the make of the car they had brought Ollie in. Why the van, then? And someone had requested that I be brought here, specifically. I blew out a breath of air. Those were questions for later.

"Have you been here long?" I said in a hushed voice.

"Not long. A couple of days maybe." A tear shone in the crook of her eye. "Hard to keep track really, and I was out for a while after they tased me."

She was just a kid. What the hell were these guys thinking?

"All right. It'll be all right."

Her eyes drooped a little. "It won't. I've seen what they do."

I didn't want to push her. At the same time, we were still alive, and as long as we were not dead, we could fight. If only I had my powers. I kept my eyes on Kaede and mused. If she was caged, then surely—

"Can you do any magic?" I asked.

Kaede shook her head, and I felt myself sagging under the weight of my own misery.

"So," I said, trying to distract the both of us. "When you're not caged like this, what power do you have?"

She said nothing.

"Close your eyes, and let's pretend we're on a beach." I closed my eyes first, then peeked out under half-open lids to find that she had closed hers as well. "Now, listen to the birds and the waves lapping gently. Feel the warmth of the sun on your skin."

Kaede raised her chin as if she was stretching for the sun. Good.

"Want to tell me now, Kaede?" I asked softly.

"Powers." Her mouth twitched into a weak smile. "Healing and force fields."

"Really?" She had powers like mine.

"It's amazing, actually. I get to help people, protect others." She bit her lip as if she had said something wrong.

"You're allowed to be proud," I said.

"I'm not supposed to share."

"Neither am I, but I won't tell if you don't."

We talked for a while longer, sharing stories about magic and everyday stuff. It seemed to help Kaede loosen up and take her mind off the pickle we were both in. She kept her eyes closed, but I couldn't. I had to stay alert. Eventually, however, my eyes refused to listen and closed shut.

# SIXTEEN

"IN THERE," A GRAVELLY VOICE SAID, SPURRING ME AWAKE.

A glass of water and a box of chicken salad stood in the corner of my cage. My lips parted, and I grabbed the glass, chugging down every last drop.

"Let me go," a boy shouted.

"Shut it!" Lionel stood two cages away from me by an open cage.

"I just want to—" The boy never got to finish his sentence. The crackling noise of electricity made me flinch as if I was the one taking the hit.

The boy was flung into the cage, the door slammed shut. Lionel searched his keychain until he found a match, and locked the door. My eyes fastened on the keychain. If I could just get out of this cage and get to those keys, then I could find Nick, and we could get the hell out of Dodge. Right. Like that would be a breezy run. As stupid as it was, it gave me a small piece of hope.

The newcomer stirred in his cage, his head lifting with obvious effort.

That face. I had stared into that face so hard these past few days; I had even seen it using my truesight. It was Oliver.

"I'm sorry, Lionel." The voice came from Ulfius this time. "It was an accident."

Lionel slapped Ulfius with the flat of his hand. Hard, though not hard enough for a knockout. "You dimwit. But keep your mouth shut, and we'll fix your mess before Mordred finds out."

"I didn't mean to taint the blood. I just wanted to test mind control for a while, but then I got the samples mixed up, and—"

"Shut your gob, Ulf."

Ulfius jumped onto one of the metal tables and held out a syringe. "We got some of his blood now. Fancy testing it?"

Were they insane? Taking unprocessed Magical blood would kill them. Idiots. Then again, a part of me hoped they were that stupid, and that they both ended up dead on the floor from heart failure.

"You absolute donkey." Lionel shook his head wildly, snatching the syringe from Ulfius' hands. "Not how it's done. There's actual processed MagX in the fridge for whenever you want to get a kick. Right now, we've got work to do."

What in seven ways to Avalon? They were users. Not that it should come as a surprise, since whoever tried to grab me in the park the other day was probably one of these men. I could feel an eye roll coming on as Lionel hauled Ulfius to his feet.

"Here." He tucked a panel into Ulfius' jeans. "For after."

The men laughed, stepping away from the cages to walk down the length of the room, and disappeared from view.

I pushed myself upright, gritting my teeth at the stiffness of my bones, and the searing pain in my back.

"Ollie," I whispered.

He quirked his head up, shifting around to meet my eyes. "How do you know my name?"

"I know Teagan. She sort of sent me to help you."

He snorted. "Yeah, a lot of good you'll do in there." He paused for a moment, his hands folding over his cheeks, his fingers resting against his brow. "How is she?"

"Worried sick about you, but alive and kicking."

"That's my Teagan." A hint of a smile lit up his face. It really was a picture-perfect face, even underneath all the dirt.

"Any idea how to get out of here, or what's going on?"

"I was here for a while before they took some blood from me for testing. Then they moved me upstairs to another cage. And just now, Ulfius came to fetch me and drag my ass back down here. Something about a bad sample, and having to check my blood again."

"But why? Are they checking to see what powers are in your blood? Can they do that?" The thought was unsettling.

"You don't know?"

"What?"

"They are checking to see how pure we are. It seems like a Pure Mag gets slightly different treatment than the rest of us. And those poor sods with next to no magic at all, well, seems they get the silencing treatment."

My hands balled up, my panic coursing back. Nick had no magic at all. Were they silencing him right now? Was he dead already? I shook myself. I had to believe Nick was alive, and that I could break out and find him.

Oliver pulled a hand through his tangled brown hair. "The bloke next to me upstairs said he's been here a week already, and there's been maybe fifty or so Mags come through, but only one Pure that he could tell."

My tired mind struggled to fit the pieces together. The water had helped, though. I grabbed the salad and stuffed my mouth. It could very well be poisoned, though why would they go through all this trouble just to poison me? Besides, I was probably going to die anyway, and I would need all the strength I could get if I were to stand any chance of avoiding that outcome.

"We should go for Lionel's keys," I mumbled.

"And how do you propose we do that? We can't spell ourselves out of these cages. And I assume your magic is working as poorly as mine at the moment." He narrowed his eyes at me. "What can you do?"

I opened my mouth to speak when Mordred stepped into the fluorescent light. It made him look bigger than I remembered. His broad shoulders were squared, his wide chin set tight. He moved closer with determined steps, stopping by Kaede's cage.

"Up!" he bellowed.

Kaede, who had been asleep, scrambled to her knees, and Mordred opened the cage door. He grabbed her arm, thrusting her out of the cage only to pin her onto the nearest table. There, he strapped her tight, her body stiff underneath the restraints.

"Get away from her," I yelled.

Mordred ignored me, his focus entirely on Kaede. "What a beautiful specimen you are," he said in a guttural voice. "Let's see what hides inside those veins, shall we?"

I couldn't see Kaede's face properly, but her whimpers tore at my heart. The whines soon turned to sobs.

"Quiet." Mordred punched his fist in her face and the sobbing ceased. The silence was almost worse than her cries, and my heart clenched in my chest. He motioned with his hand, and the door to Kaede's cage slammed shut.

Holy Lady. He was drugged out of his mind. On what, though? Some Telekinetic's blood was my best bet.

I yelped before anger flared back inside. But no fire. I needed my fire. I pushed and searched, and tried everything to find it, but there was no trace of a response from the magic inside.

Oliver regarded me with low-set brows. "It won't work," he said under his breath. "Human blood." He drew his sleeve up, and I could just about make out a puncture wound on his arm.

Looking down, I found two puncture wounds on my own skin. They had injected me with human blood, assuming Oliver was right. Something clicked in my brain as I remembered the syringe Jen had found back when we were looking for Ilyana. It had human blood in it.

"Why?" I said.

"Neutralises our powers."

Defeated, I put my forehead in my hands, still glancing up to look at the scene in front of me. Oliver was right. There was nothing I could do. And I hated the feeling. I had no idea how human blood in my system worked, but I hoped it would wear off. And soon.

Mordred moved around Kaede. His hand buried itself into her hair, and he jerked her head up as far as it would go against the restraints.

She gave a low sobbing sound that stopped moments later.

"I think I'll just have a little taste before we ship you upstairs."

I found myself on my knees, as close to the bars as I could get. A taste? He was as mad as Ulfius, or maybe madder.

"That'll kill him," I whispered.

"Not if he's already on PureX," mumbled Oliver. "By the looks of him, I'd say he's had a fix before coming here."

I didn't understand. I did remember what I had learned about PureX, however. It was the most recent addition to the Magical drug market. My gaze moved back to the scene in front of me as Mordred's shadow fell over Kaede.

"Your blood samples came back with a very interesting result. We don't get a lot of Fae in here, and certainly not someone Pure."

I stiffened, my hands dropping. Her powers had been a dead giveaway that she was Fae—like me—only she was a Pure. And I was stuck in a cage, unable to help her. I had never known another Fae besides my mum, my grandparents excluded since I only knew them from Mum's stories. And Mum was the only other Pure I knew as well.

Mordred held up a syringe, then drew the edge of the needle down Kaede's face and over her chest, down to her stomach. That bastard. He was playing with her. His face distorted into a wicked grin as he paused, the needle now resting right below Kaede's rib cage.

"This will take too long," he muttered, more to himself than anyone else. Placing the syringe on a smaller metal table, he picked up something else. It was thin, with a sharp edge. I sucked in a breath as I recognised the instrument from Mum's clinic. It was a scalpel.

Kaede's muscles tensed, her veins showing through the skin on her arms. She was so thin.

"Easy, kitten." Mordred brought the scalpel down, sliding it into Kaede's wrist and slicing it up the length of her forearm.

Blood. Streams of blood gushed from the open wound. Mordred's cold eyes glimmered with excitement. He bent down and licked his tongue across the wound. His head craned back, and he made a sound of satisfaction, a low grunt in his chest. Then he laughed, his head snapping back. Blood smeared his lips.

Kaede was writhing under the bonds keeping her down.

"You have to close her up," I screamed.

"What a rush," Mordred said, a vicious grin on his face. "I need more."

"You have to stop the bleeding!"

It was as if he didn't hear me at all. Instead, he licked the wound again, blood now running down his chin and neck, dripping onto the floor. I tried to summon fire again—desperately reaching for what I knew was there—somewhere. Yet again, I couldn't reach it.

Kaede convulsed with short intervals as a scarlet pool spread underneath the table she lay on.

I started crying. The tears streamed uncontrollably down my face. "Help her!"

Mordred puffed himself up, flexing his arms, then he pushed his palms out, and the cage Kaede had occupied lifted from the ground to spin in the air. He flicked his fingers this way and that, the bars of the cage bending and breaking, eventually turning into a metal ball, twisted with shards and spikes sticking out. He continued to lift the ball all the way to the ceiling before he sent it crashing to the ground with full force. It slammed downwards.

My heart jumped as the metal ball thundered into the ground next to me, the concrete cracking at the impact before the ball jammed itself about two feet into the ground. The floor shook violently, ringing metal issuing all around me, and the cage bars crackled with sparks of blue light. Metal shards ricocheted through the air. I cried out in pain as one of the shards came through the bars, tearing at my arm in passing. Finally, the room stilled.

Mordred proceeded as if nothing had happened. He collected a bunch of vials and began filling them with Kaede's blood before he placed them into a small rack. He walked over to open the steel doors, and a cold gust breezed over me. He stepped inside for a short while, and came back out without the rack, shutting the door behind him. Picking up another vial as he went, he paused mid-step to look at Kaede. He pocketed the vial he was holding and shook his head.

"Aw, fuck," he mumbled, placing two fingers to her neck. He wiped his face, leaving stripes of red over his cheeks and the bridge of his nose. "You had to go die on me, didn't you? Blasted Mags."

I sniffled, blinking hard against the tears. Kaede was gone.

Mordred sighed heavily, lifted his hands and gestured at the table. It rattled and lifted from the ground before Mordred lumbered off, pushing the table in front of him through the air. Somewhere far in the distance, a door opened and shut, and then they were gone.

I curled up inside the cage, unable to stop the tears from falling. Weeping, I hugged myself and wished I had never gone to London at all, that I had never seen the things I had. Most of all, I wished Kaede didn't have to die. I thought I had known what Harvesters did, what they were. In my stupidity, I thought I could stay out of their path and live my life like any normal young woman. But I wasn't normal, and I couldn't unsee what I'd seen. And if I ever got out of here, I would stop at nothing to wipe these 'Sentries of Camelot', or whatever they called themselves, from the face of the Earth, along with any Harvesting worm I could find.

# SEVENTEEN

"FOUND IT," ULFIUS CALLED, HIS GANGLY FORM SWAYING forwards. He held a syringe in the air and waved it carelessly above his head before placing it on a small table.

Lionel searched his keychain. He stopped, separating one key from the others, and proceeded to jam it into the keyhole of my cage before flinging the door open. I backed up on my toes, as close to the bars as I dared to get. I could feel a hint of my powers again. It wasn't much, but it was there. The fire inside snaked around my bones, and my veins pulsated with anticipation.

Ulfius leaned past Lionel and inserted his head into the cage. He reached for my arm. I sucked in a breath and placed my palm forward, willing the flames to come out.

They didn't. It was there, fizzing away in my veins. But it wasn't strong enough.

I wasn't.

A calloused, sweaty hand closed around my wrist,

forcing me to tumble forward out of the cage. I raised my arm to attack when he grabbed my other wrist as well, and I kicked my feet into nothing but air. He locked my arms behind my back, lifting me onto one of the metal tables.

"Hold her still," Lionel hissed.

"Should have done this when she was unconscious like last time," Ulfius breathed through gritted teeth. "She's mighty strong."

"We have to do it at the set time, or the last dosage will have gone out of her system, you bonehead. Keep her down."

I struggled, my feet hammering against the metal. On any other day, I was sure I could have taken Ulfius. As it was, I was too tired, too weak—too human.

The needle of the syringe glinted at the edge of my vision and I tried twisting away from it. It came down, the tip of it pressing against my forearm. It didn't break the skin, however, as Lionel toppled to the side, thumping to the ground with the syringe sliding away and across the floor. I shifted my gaze around.

A familiar face stared at me. Nick! He was alive!

He stood with a massive steel rod in his hand, grinning like a fool—the best kind. The hold on my arms loosened as Ulfius let go. He veered around my side and rammed his body into Nick. They sprawled on the ground, fists slamming into one another.

Sliding off the table, I steadied my feet, ready to lunge forward. When I found my balance, I rushed over to help Nick. My foot caught on the steel rod Nick had used and sent me sailing to the floor. I braced myself, thrusting my palms out for protection.

A surge of exhilarating magic filled me up before a force field spread out underneath me, alleviating the impact.

I smiled broadly. My powers were coming back. How long until they were at full force, I had no idea, but at least they responded to my calling.

With a swing of my hands, I rolled sideways and flung the force field out to wrap around Nick. Ulfius went for him but staggered back as he hit the field. He stumbled, diving back into the shards of metal protruding from the ball left behind by Mordred. Two sharp spikes shot through his abdomen, leaving him skewered on the ball. I shuddered as I watched the blood gush out of his jerking body.

Something caught my eye, and I spun into a crouch. Lionel was on his feet, steadying himself on the metal table where I had just been. A purplish lump grew on his bald head. He glowered at me, then lifted one hand, holding a small device with a large red button on it. He swung his palm over it and pressed the device between his hands.

The shriek of an alarm wailed through the building, and flashes of red light erupted along the walls. My heart raced. We had to get out now.

Lionel dropped the device and drew a gun from its holster. I hadn't even noticed it before. I had been too preoccupied with everything else. Looking straight into the barrel, much the same way as I had back at the skatepark, I reacted on instinct.

The gun went off as I ripped the force field from Nick, sending it flying forwards, trapping the bullet and Lionel inside. The bullet bounced into the field, surged back, and drove a hole into Lionel's arm.

My anger flared into life, in spades this time. Burning, white-hot, like the fire I possessed. I squeezed my hands together, making the force field tighten around Lionel. Sprays of blood painted the veil of the field a crimson red. Tighter. I kept pushing until the force field was plastered around Lionel. He gasped for air that wasn't there anymore. His mouth opened wide, his chest heaving rapidly. Then his breathing slowed, and the rising of his chest began to die down.

"Ruby," Nick yelled. "We have to go."

I vaguely registered Nick's voice as I kept the force field up, waiting for Lionel to take his last breath. I didn't stop until I was certain he was dead.

"Ruby!" Nick put a hand on my shoulder.

I flinched, letting go of the force field. Lionel crashed to the floor, and this time he wasn't getting back up.

"The alarm, Ruby," Nick said.

I raised my eyes to him, slowly aware of the sound of a siren still blaring all around us. "Oliver! We have to get him out first."

I crouched down next to Lionel. Without care for the dead man, I wiggled the keychain away from his belt and ran for Oliver's cage.

My hands were shaking as I tried to find the right key, and twice I dropped the keychain to the floor.

"Hurry up," Oliver whispered desperately. "That monster could come back at any time."

I had no desire to stay a second longer than I had to, Mordred being one of the top reasons. Behind me, Nick had grabbed the steel rod and stood guard, bless him. If Mordred came, he would stand no chance. How in the name of the Lady had Nick escaped?

A click in the lock told me I'd found the right key. I swung the cage door open, carefully at first, not knowing if I would be hit by an electric shock. I sighed in relief when no buzzing came. Oliver had no intention of being careful, however, and burst out of the cage.

"Easy." I nodded in the direction Mordred had left earlier. "I think he has some kind of power over metal. We can't take him on. Not yet, at least."

"Are your powers back?" Oliver asked.

"Yeah, but not at full force by far. And you?"

"I think I was due for another shot of human blood," he said, "but by the looks of it, room service is out of order. Well done!"

"Thanks." Nick patted Oliver on his shoulder. "Ah, you meant her."

"I meant both of you. Now, let's hang on to the small talk until we're out of here. Follow me."

He ran past the metal ball and up the stairs. Nick followed him, and I deliberately waited to have him between Oliver and me. I owed him my life and was dead set on keeping him safe.

I glanced at Ulfius as I passed him. The convulsions had stopped, and his eyes had lost the last gleam of life.

He had clearly been at the lowest level of whatever hierarchy this twisted group operated under. I almost felt sorry for him.

At the top of the stairs, Oliver turned left.

"Wait," I said. "We need to free the others." I looked the other way, towards the cages—at least ten or twelve on each side of the gangway.

"We'll get caught," Oliver said. "There are lots of guards, and as soon as they see the chaos downstairs, we're screwed. We need help."

"He's right, Ruby." Nick glanced back over his shoulder. "Let's get out of here and phone—whoever we need to phone."

I knew they were right, but leaving the others behind felt wrong. Deadly wrong.

Oliver ran on, with Nick close behind him. I had no choice but to follow. Oliver stopped by a door at the end of the gangway and opened it carefully, taking a peek at the other side. He waved at Nick and me, holding the door open.

"Look out!" Oliver shouted as I dashed through the opening, my foot catching the threshold. I fell forward and landed on my stomach, just as a loud, screeching sound echoed off the walls, immediately followed by an even louder crash. Fragments of the doorframe rained over me, needles of pain stinging my neck. When I looked up, the steel door that Oliver had so carefully opened was nailed to the opposite wall with a ten-foot steel bar. Something—or someone—had ripped it off its hinges and flung it across the room like a frisbee.

I got to my knees and turned to look for the others.

Oliver threw himself through the opening, almost landing on top of me.

"They're in the upper hall. Get them!" a familiar voice thundered from outside the opening. Mordred. If he was still juiced up on PureX, he'd have us in no time.

As Nick and Oliver ran through the empty hall towards a double door at the end, I dropped to all fours and crawled back towards the doorway behind us. I peeked through, and almost gasped at the sight. At the top of the stairs, where the three of us had stood not more than thirty seconds earlier, Mordred turned towards me. Hoping beyond hope that my instincts were right, that my powers increased every second now that the human blood no longer had a hold on them, I called upon the fire inside.

Mordred reached out his left arm, and the screeching sound of metal being bent penetrated my ears. From the corner of my eye, I could see the top bars on the guardrail curl like spaghetti. I had one chance, and one chance only.

My magic surged through my body so hard that I almost lifted off the floor and, with all my strength, I flung a giant fireball towards Mordred. The room was bathed in crimson from the rotating lights, but when my fire released from my hands, the heat was so intense it shattered them all. My head was spinning with emotion, the ecstatic joy of having my powers flow through me balancing against the anger towards the monsters who had captured me—and the other victims. As the flames died down, the room fell dark red again, dimly lit by glowing crimson lines along the walls.

Mordred had managed to rip one of the guardrails free and flung it towards me at lightning speed. Before it could reach me, however, the fire melted it. I ducked to avoid the melted steel, but all that was left was a scorched cloud of vapour rising to the ceiling.

I looked at the chaos I had caused. The gangway we had run across was gone. I tried to recall if any of the cages had been close, but was almost certain they were all further back.

*Oh, Lady of Avalon, don't let any of the Mags have fallen victim to my fire!*

The inferno I had released hadn't just melted the steel gangway and guardrails, so much as totally evaporated it. Tiny, glowing red drops fell from the remaining structure and onto the floor below.

Of Mordred, there was nothing left.

My thoughts were soon interrupted by gunshots behind me.

I spun around, leapt to my feet, and sprinted towards the double doors. If Nick had been shot, I would never forgive myself.

A bullet pierced the door frame next to my head, splinters of wood flying before my eyes. The doors led to a corridor, and about twenty yards ahead, a terrible sight met me. Nick and Oliver lay splayed on the floor.

Bullets kept whizzing through the corridor from the other end, past the boys, barrelling into the walls and ceiling. I threw a force field down the corridor, pulling it outwards to block the shooting guards from my friends on the floor. There were two sentries, and now they had stepped into the corridor, guns raised. Their bullets bounced off the force field.

How long could I maintain it? I had already spent a lot of my magical energy on Mordred. I reached Nick and Oliver, who were still on the floor, shielding themselves with their hands.

"Are you ok?" I shouted over roaring blasts of gunshots.

"I—I think so," Nick replied. "Although that's a creative use of the term ok."

A bullet zinged past me, burying itself in the wall at the end of the corridor. I was losing control of the force field. How could we get out of here, trapped between the shooters and what I assumed were more sentries coming from behind us any moment? They would be slowed down by the wrecked gangway, but I didn't want to wait to find out how much.

The guard on the left made the decision for me when he turned his gun at his colleague. He pulled the trigger, and I threw my hands in front of my face a fraction of a second too late. The image of the guard's head exploding, leaving a gaping hole where his forehead should be, was forever imprinted on my brain. What on earth had made the other guard shoot him?

I looked at Oliver; his arm was outstretched, his lips curved up. What had convinced the guard was not of this Earth at all. Oliver had made him turn on his colleague, using his mind control. Now, he tilted his head ever so slightly to the left, a grin drawing wide on his face.

"Had to try, as I don't think that shield of yours is of any use no more."

He was right. It was no bigger than half the width of the corridor.

I looked at the remaining guard. His colleague had slumped to the floor. The last one standing stared at Oliver with desperation and terror in his eyes. His face twisted into a frightening grimace as he realised what I had concluded seconds earlier.

"Don't!" I screamed. "Please, Oliver!"

The guard clearly tried to fight it as his hand turned towards his head. His eyes shifted from Oliver to the gun. I couldn't let this happen.

A loud crack echoed through the corridor when a bright flash erupted from the muzzle. It spread like fireworks on New Year's Eve onto the force field I had thrown at the guard's head, pulling my last bit of magic out of me. A sizzling noise followed as the bullet ricocheted off the field, and hit the ceiling above him. Dust and debris landed atop the nearly invisible globe.

Nick reacted in an instant, running towards the guard with his steel rod raised. "Let go of the field, Ruby!" he shouted.

I did as he told me. Not so much because I wanted to, but because my powers had drained my energy a lot.

Nick struck the guard on his knees, and he fell like a bad guy in a Jason Statham flick. In one quick motion, Nick had pried the gun from his hands, and pointed it at the guard, underlining the Statham image. I'd have to tell him later, I thought, as I sprinted towards them.

"We can't leave him alive," Oliver said.

"Don't worry," Nick said. "He won't be a problem." He swung the steel bar at the poor sod's head, and the impact made a sickening crunch.

"Oops. I tried not to kill him," Nick said, looking at the bloody gash at the back of the guard's head.

I crouched, feeling with my fingers for a pulse. I sent a tiny amount of healing into the man, not sure how much, if anything, I had left in me. Maybe it would keep him alive, but not revive him. "He'll be fine," I said.

"This is where they brought me inside." Oliver pointed at a side door. "Let's split."

I got my first hint at the time of day when we opened the door. The time of night, at least. It was freezing and above us, the stars and a quarter slice of the moon threw an eerie light from the clear sky. We cleared the three or four steps down to the ground and sprinted towards the silhouettes of trees across the field.

My mind was fixed on reaching the woods, but also on turning back to save the rest of the caged Magicals.

What little light the moon and the stars provided helped us find the treeline. We couldn't risk running any further, however, as crashing into a trunk would be devastating.

"Stop," I whispered as loud as I could without actually shouting.

We had come at least fifty yards into the woods, and when I turned to look, the farm and buildings were lost in the dark.

"We need to think," I said, as the boys came towards me. "Also, we need to gather more power."

"We have no chance alone, Ruby," Oliver said. "I mean, that fire thing you do is great and all, but it's clear your batteries are almost out of juice. We need to phone for help."

"How?" I said. "They took my phone, and I'm guessing you're not exactly stocked like an Apple Store yourself?"

"No," he said. "They rook mine ash—"

Something was wrong. "Oliver?" I reached out to grab his arm.

"I thing I'm hurr—" he slurred, his eyes rolling back in their sockets. His knees buckled, and he fell to the ground, dragging me down with him.

"He's hit." Nick dropped to his knees next to Oliver. "Look." He pointed at Oliver's neck. A dark inch-wide patch had formed on his skin. In the dim light, the blood running down his chest was oily black.

I leaned in to have a closer look. With my hands cupped to shield the light, I lit a tiny flame, praying to The Lady of the Lake that it couldn't be spotted from the farm.

It was bad. Really bad.

"He must have been hit by a gunshot," Nick muttered. "Is the bullet still in there?"

"I don't know," I said. "I hope not. I've never treated any gunshot wounds before."

"Treated? As in ...?"

I didn't answer. I lay my hand on top of the wound, swallowing to keep from gagging as Oliver's warm blood pulsated underneath my palm. The bullet must have grazed the aorta, which had stayed intact for a few minutes–but now it had ruptured.

Mum once told me she had been in the line of cars behind a speeding BMW, and when the driver decided to wrap the car around a tree, Mum had sprinted towards him, ignoring the flames that threatened to reach the gas tank. She hadn't been able to save him, however, as his aorta was torn to pieces.

Juice or no juice, I emptied whatever magic energy I had left in me into Oliver's neck, the intoxicating rush of healing flowed through me. It was nothing like the rage I felt when I used my fire, or the calmness releasing a force field filled me with. Healing was my favourite power, simply because of this exact experience. I closed my eyes, even though that had no effect on the power itself. It did, however, enhance the colours that danced before my inner vision.

Oliver's body jerked beneath my hand. He coughed and sputtered, and I opened my eyes to see his gaze meet mine. Ok, this was also quite a rush, watching the effect my healing had on people.

Oliver sat, his torso swaying a little.

"Whoa, there," said Nick, throwing his arm around Oliver to steady him. "Let's not get ahead of ourselves."

I smiled, knowing all too well how wrong he was. Oliver helped prove my unspoken point when he shook Nick's arm away and got to his feet.

"Are you kidding?" he said, a bit too loud. "Sorry," he whispered. "But are you fucking kidding me?"

He stared at me, then at my hands. "That's —that's—"

I shrugged and stifled a laugh. "I know," I whispered. "He's fine, Nick. Don't worry."

We sat in silence, looking at each other and glancing back towards the farm every now and then.

The image of Lionel started forming in my head. Again and again, I watched his agonizing look as he realised what was happening. I could have let go of the force field earlier. He would've fainted from lack of oxygen. But I kept it going—wanted to keep it going. Forcing it tighter and tighter. It felt good. I had thought of Kaede as I tightened it way beyond what I had to in order to kill him. I only wished I had squashed his head completely. What was this? I had never felt such rage before. Rage and ... a dark desire to kill my enemies.

"Ruby?"

"Huh?"

"What's up?" Nick said, holding my shoulders and looking into my eyes. "You're literally fuming!"

I raised my hand, touching my cheek. Tears flowed from my eyes, but they turned into steam before reaching halfway down my face. I shook my head, trying to calm down. "I killed him," I said. "Lionel."

"You had to," Nick said.

"No, I didn't have to kill him. But I did."

*And I wanted to!*

"Ru, look at me. You had no choice."

*But I did. And I chose to suffocate him.*

"Oliver? She had no choice, right?"

Oliver didn't answer.

"Oliver?"

We turned, both Nick and I. Oliver was staring towards the farm.

"What?" I said, trying to see through the darkness. "Did you hear anything?"

"No," he said. "And that worries me. I don't want to sound like a cliché, but it's too quiet. There are at least twenty guards in that ... facility. We took out two of them."

"Five," I said. "Ulfius and Lionel, remember? And Mordred."

"You killed Mordred?" Nick was gaping at me.

"He's no longer with us," I replied.

"Ok, five then," Oliver continued. "That leaves at least fifteen. Fully armed, probably stocking their bloodstreams with PureX as we speak. God only knows what powers they'll have."

A chill crept down my spine, and I wrapped my arms around myself, shuddering at the thought as much as the cold air.

"We've got to keep going," Oliver said. "Get as far away as we can before they come for us."

"What about phoning for help?" I said.

"How? Care to light the forest on fire, and send some smoke signals, perhaps?"

"We could use this." Nick waved a phone in his hand. "It's not the fruity kind, but a Samsung might do the job, too."

"Where did you get that?" I said. "And why didn't you say so before?"

"I did a little lift. Sort of a magic trick. And for your

information, I've been kinda busy lately, trying not to get killed."

"Sorry," I said. "You're right, of course. Give me the phone, I know who to—"

Five sharp cracks thundered through the clear night as two giant searchlights flooded the forest in bright white cylinders of light.

"Get down!" Oliver hissed.

The beams swiped from side to side, flickering through the trees like a strobe at an 80s revival party. Shadows danced through the beams, getting closer and closer. Shadows in the shape of men.

Men with guns and magical powers.

# EIGHTEEN

A VOICE BARKED ORDERS THROUGH THE NIGHT.

"Left flank—you two!"

"Bedivere and Tristan, to the right."

"The rest—with me in the centre!"

The next order sent chills through my blood.

"Use lethal force!"

From my crouched position behind the closest trunk I had found, I could just make out the dark outline of Nick's body as he crawled like a snake towards me. Judging by the movement of the search-light beams, the sentries hadn't spotted us. Yet.

"I can't reach their minds from here," Oliver whispered in my left ear. "I have to be closer."

"They'll kill you if you try," I replied. "Stay low. And quiet!"

More orders echoed through the darkness. I had no idea how fast my magic powers regenerated, or how much the human blood held them back. The longer I waited, the stronger I became, but every waiting breath gave the guards a chance to home in on us.

"I've got one!" someone shouted.

A fraction of a second later, the sound of a gunshot split the night, a thin whistle as a bullet passed over my head.

"Oy, wanker! That was one of mine!" shouted someone else. "I've got three of me out here! Shoot the runaways instead, four-eyes."

What did he mean, three of him? Was he a—? The word wouldn't come to me. Mum had told me about Magicals who could make copies of themselves, some sort of astral projection. The perfect decoys in a combat situation. One of his colleagues must have fired at one of the copies. Splitters, wasn't that what Mum had called them?

These guards had access to a whole arsenal of magical powers—weapons in the wrong hands. I couldn't wait any longer, or we'd be sitting ducks.

"I'll distract them. Run that way in five seconds," I whispered to Nick, loud enough for Oliver to pick it up. "Run, and don't stop!" As I had feared, my voice carried further than intended.

"Two o'clock! Light 'em up!"

Like spotlights at a rock concert, the beams centred on us.

"Go!" I snapped to the boys.

As their shadows vanished from the deceitful lights, I tried calling upon my firepower. As I heaved for air, with a pounding pain in my arm, I almost gave up when nothing happened. Please, let there be some left.

Again, Gabriel's words came floating through my mind:

'Anyone can tap into their magical reserves and harness their full potential. It's all about self-control.'

So far, all he had said about my magic was true. Maybe this was, as well? I closed my eyes and drew my breath, calling once more to the red-hot core of my powers. The response came, weak at first, but growing. Simmering. It was as if it called back to me, urging me to use it.

I dove out from my hiding place, turned in the air and released a giant fireball, watching it rush towards the silhouettes.

The fireball hammered the ground like a bomb, its blast wave throwing me backwards. I had no time to release a force field, but the soft mossy ground made the impact tolerable. My fireball had made quite an impact, too, as the remaining trees in at least a fifty-foot radius were ablaze. Screams from burning guards reached me as I worked my way back on my feet. One guard was running in my direction, his feet leaving fiery footprints on the forest floor. As he fell to his knees, some twenty or more steps away from me, the stench of his burning flesh made my stomach heave. His face contorted with fear and pain until it was no longer a face at all, but a skull with slivers of melting meat and skin.

I still had no idea if I could throw fire from inside a force field, and didn't want to waste time trying to find out. As long as there was fire left in me, however, it would be my weapon of choice.

I got up on one knee as a trio of guards came running at me from the left. They looked identical in the strobing change between darkness and light beams. Tristan and Bedivere, I recalled—and the one who gave the orders. They raised their guns to their shoulders in a perfectly synchronized motion. Bullets whizzed past me, hitting the ground and trees left and right.

With both hands in front of me, I returned the fire —literally. Tiny, luminous balls gushed out of my palms as I pushed my marksmanship to the edge. I clearly saw one of them hit the gunman straight in his chest, but he didn't fall. Instead, the image of him vanished in thin air. I had found one of the Splitter's copies.

Screw the finesse, then. No time for guessing which one of the remaining images was the real deal. I held my hands up, palms outward, spreading a barrage of devouring flames in front of me. Jumping through the wall of fire came only one, the real one. His body landed with a sickening thud on the ground, sending sparks and burning pieces of the former officer into the scorched grass.

I turned my hands towards the ground, pushing a force field downwards as hard as I could. The shock sent me flying through the air. For the tiniest of moments, I had a bird's eye view of the battleground; at least six or seven guards—or what remained of them— lay in flames in the giant crater my fireball had made.

I whirled through the air, pulling the force field towards me, and managed to wrap it around me before I landed, more than twenty-five yards from where I'd taken off. There were only two guards left, and they hadn't fixed their guns on me. Big mistake. This Mag had more in store for them. I let go of the force field and loaded my hands with more fire. The adrenalin was fuelling my powers.

A bone-shattering pain sent spasms through my body, throwing me to the ground, face down. My body shook as the familiar electricity surged through me. I tried to reach for my magic, but it wouldn't respond. Small lines of fire ran in the grass from my hands, ignited by the remaining heat that I no longer could control.

"That's it, you Maggot. You're done here!"

He spun me to my back like a ragdoll. In his hand was a black rod, maybe four feet long, with me attached to the end by a metal wire around my neck. I'd seen them on TV, dog catchers or even crocodile hunters used them. I was defenceless, spitting moss and sand as I tried to fix my gaze on him.

His eyes widened, the sheer madness glaring at me. "Mordred wanted you for himself, little'un. Seeing what you've done to my colleagues—my friends—I think I'll have to disappoint him."

I ignored his words and tried to reach my magic. He pushed the button on the rod, sending another jolt of electricity through my limp body. As his lips parted and drew into a rabid grin, drops of saliva fell on my arm.

"No more magic for you, I'm afraid." His voice had turned into a mix between a hissing snake and a roaring tiger. He let go of the rod with his right hand and drew a pistol from the holster on his hip.

"Sleep tight."

I stared into the black void of the muzzle, bracing for what I hoped would be quick and painless.

A loud growl split the air, but it was not the sentry who screamed. Our eyes met, his shock written on his face. Before any of us could react, he was thrown sideways by a huge, white, furry mass.

The wire around my neck loosened, and I grabbed it to pull it over my head. A few feet to my left, the forest floor turned red. The guard lay on the ground, frantically trying to fight off the snapping mouth that had already ripped huge chunks of meat from his torso.

The wolf glanced at me, and I swore I could see a question in her eyes.

I nodded. "I'm ok, Jen."

Jen returned to ripping the guard to pieces, only letting up when his head no longer could be counted as part of him. It dangled by a thin sinew from Jen's blood-soaked fangs, two feet above the pulp that once had been a man. Jen shook her head, like a dog playing with a sock, causing the head to fly sideways, coming to rest somewhere in the darkness.

"Behind you!" I shouted.

A muzzle flame lit up from behind a tree. Jen let out a howl and pounced for the shooter. I finally managed to free myself from the loop and the pole and got to my knees. Jen was almost at the tree, hurling herself at the guard. As she landed atop him, her canines penetrated his eye sockets.

"Look out, Nick!" Oliver yelled behind me.

They hadn't got away. Jen seemed to have every-thing under control—if tearing into a grown man's rib cage with one's forepaws could be described as control. I turned and dashed towards Oliver's voice. I heard no gunshots, which had to be a good sign. Didn't it?

It wasn't. At the outskirts of the treeline, Nick and Oliver were fighting off a six-foot-five policeman in full uniform. The copper swung his nightstick repeatedly at Nick, who fended off each blow with an iron rod like a knight with his sword.

Oliver sat on the ground, his hands pressing against his temples. Was he hurt? Or was he trying to get into the copper's head?

I didn't plan on waiting to find out. The effects of the electric shocks had died down, and I could sense my powers boosting in my core. With a surge of magic —and quite a bit of adrenalin—I pushed a force field towards Nick without missing a step. As the field enclosed him, the copper stopped his forehand practice and turned to face me.

I prepared to launch a fireball at him, but some-thing in his eyes changed. Shifted. From anger to fear— no, confusion.

"You'll want this," the policeman said, throwing the nightstick at my feet. "I can sit here." He crouched, dusted the grass with his hand, and sat. "He will put my cuffs on now." He pointed at Oliver, who leaned over him, opened the little black holster, and took the handcuffs.

Oliver smiled at me, swaying a little. Sweat trickled down his temple.

"I've got him," he said. "But not for long."

The policeman amiably moved his hands behind his back, and Oliver clicked the cuffs in place, before falling flat on the grass.

"Ollie!" I dropped to my knees next to him. "Are you hurt?"

"Tis but a flesh wound," he moaned, giving me a crooked smile. "Get it?"

"I do. The Black Knight. Fitting," I said, nodding at the farm. "I guess we've found Camelot."

I lay my hand on his chest, ready to send my healing into his body, but he pushed me away.

"Really, I'm fine. Save your energy. This isn't over yet."

He was right, of course. There were lots of Mags inside, and I had no intention of leaving them there for a minute more than needed.

"How many guards, you reckon?" I said.

"How many did we get?"

"I think there are four or five in the woods, and the five from before. And this vegetable, of course." I nodded at the very cooperative policeman; PC Spencer, according to the name tag on his chest pocket.

"He came up the road," Nick said. "Care to let me out of this soap bubble?"

I had forgotten about the force field, which puzzled me, as I could feel no strain on my stamina. I released my hold on it.

"Oliver had another guy shoot himself, but only after the guard knocked him hard on the head. Bet you've got a nice concussion there, mate."

"Not unlikely. Took me a while to get into this guy's brain because of it. Got a serious hangover now." He turned to the policeman again.

PC Spencer flinched, then nodded slowly. "I was on my way to the morning shift. I am early because my girlfriend and I had a fight last night and I couldn't sleep. I will break up with her when I get home." His eyes shone, and a tear threatened to fall from one corner. "I should have left her long ago."

"When do the rest of the morning shift get here?" I asked.

Spencer looked at his watch. "In about an hour and a half."

Oliver shook his head, and the copper gasped as the invisible cable connecting their brains snapped.

"Wow, that's not something you see every day," Nick said.

At first, I thought he was talking about the impressive mind-controlling show Oliver had put on, but his eyes were looking at something behind me. I turned.

What had become one of my absolute favourite sights over the past weeks came trotting out of the tree-line. Jen was still in her magnificent wolf form, blood splatters all over her white fur. In her mouth, the large canines glimmered in what had become the early morning light.

"Gentlemen, meet my little pet," I said.

A low growl of discontent rumbled in her throat.

"Sorry, you're right," I said. "Neither little nor pet."

For some reason, it seemed appropriate to stroke Jen's fur, like I would a dog, something I'd never done before. She looked at me with large blue eyes, squinting ever so slightly. I interpreted it as approval and scratched her behind the ear. Her tail wagged gently from side to side.

"He's amazing," Nick said. "What's his name?"

"We'll get to that." A weak smile tugged at the corners of my mouth. "So, Oliver, want to take a wild stab at a number? How many guards left?"

"The searchlights aren't moving anymore," he said, "so that's probably a couple who've gone down off the roof. Not sure if they need one per spot, but still. Maybe five more inside. Or more."

"Between five and ten, then?" I said. "Armed and drugged up."

He shrugged. "Give or take."

"Guess we have our work cut out," I said.

"Guess so," Nick said. "Wait, what?"

I let out a little laugh. "We, as in me and the wolf. And I won't let those poor Mags sit in their cages with a bunch of gun-toting knights of the friggin' round table in there."

"Right. No, of course not," Nick said.

"You stay put here, though. Ollie too. For protection."

"Who's going to protect whom?" Oliver said. "For a human, this guy isn't too shabby."

Jen walked between the boys, stopping to sniff Oliver. Her tail stopped wagging.

"He's hurt, I know," I said.

Oliver raised his eyebrows. "It can tell?"

"To be fair, Stevie Wonder could see that you're out

of commission, mate," Nick said. "As much as I hate you going back, Ruby, I see why you have to. I'll keep brainy-boy here company." Patting Oliver on the shoulder, he made himself comfortable next to him. "Just don't go digging in my head or anything."

Oliver sighed. "Don't think I could if I tried. Be careful, Ruby."

"We will. Find someplace to hide, and if we don't come out ... well, run like Forrest Gump!"

I got to my feet and scratched Jen behind her ear. "We've got some Mags to free. Ready, sweetie?"

# NINETEEN

THE FLUSH OF THE MORNING HAD GIVEN US MORE LIGHT, which was both good news and bad. The good being that I could get a clearer picture of our surroundings. From our vantage point next to the forest, or what was left of it, I counted three buildings. A gravel road led up to the farmhouse, which probably served as sleeping quarters for the guards. Outside the house, three cars stood parked. Two vans, one of which most likely had transported Nick and me here yesterday. Or was it two days ago? I had no concept of time, other than the fact that a new day was on the horizon. Tuesday?

Behind the farmhouse was a long building that looked like stables. It made sense since there were remnants of an obstacle course in the fields further back.

And then there was the barn. It was by far the largest building, which had probably once housed a large number of cows, pigs, and whatever animals this farm had before. Before the Sentries of Camelot had acquired it and turned it into this medieval nightmare in a 21st-century wrapping, with cages and labs, and blood extracting contraptions.

The bad news was that the increasing visibility was also to our disadvantage, as we could very well find ourselves live targets for trigger-happy coppers. No reason to wait any longer.

"Let's go," I whispered in Jen's ear.

We crossed the open field as quickly as we could, which meant she had to wait for me on the other side. When I caught up, she looked back at Nick and Oliver, nodding her snout for me to look as well. They had retreated to some bushes at the edge of the forest. Good!

A whooshing sound and a gust of wind made me turn back in time to witness the final part of her shifting. If I lived to be a hundred, I'd never get used to the sight. Or stop being amazed by it.

"Hey, Red. What's up?"

I nearly broke down, but my mind couldn't decide between a laughing fit or crying.

"Where's the cat?" she asked.

"Huh?"

"The one that's got your tongue, no?"

"Sorry, I'm just so insanely happy to see you! Both in and out of your furry attire."

I realised the double entendre, as she was buck naked, but she just waved it off.

"I'll shift back soon. I just needed to talk to you, and even though I can hear and understand you while rocking wolfie style, I have no way of communicating with you." Her face shifted from the playful to the serious Jen. "What's the situation?"

"You heard our estimation on the number of guards, and they're most likely higher than the Empire State on PureX."

"PureX?"

"MagX times a hundred," I said.

"And we want to fight them because—?"

"Because they're keeping dozens of Mags in cages in there. And I fear they might employ some scorched-earth tactics, killing off all the Mags. I could be wrong, but I don't want to risk it."

"Ah, ok," Jen said in her everyday manner. "Then we free them, cool."

I turned my palms up and drew a skewed smile at her. "Basically, yes."

"TTYL." Jen wiggled her eyebrows and shifted back.

"So," I said, trying to sound casual. "It's a laundromat as well. How convenient."

Her fur had no signs of the blood splatters, and her giant canines looked fresh from the dentist. Her eyes were icy blue, with pitch dark centres. She winked at me—maybe she blinked with both eyes and I just imagined it being such a human thing as a wink— and started towards the door I had so gladly run out of a little while ago.

I followed her, keeping as close to the wall as possible, making sure nobody could spot us from the narrow windows. When we reached the door, Jen stopped. Her ears turned towards the opening like radar receptors, while her snout twitched up and down as she sniffed the air. She seemed content that nobody was inside. I wanted to encapsulate her with a force field, but as I would likely need all the energy I had in my magic storage, I had to trust she could fend for herself.

We entered the corridor and proceeded with stealthy steps towards the large hall. Halfway there, we had to cross over the unconscious guard and his headless colleague. I had to focus not to slip in the large pool of blood surrounding them, and Jen got to the double doors before me. Again, she stopped, sniffed and listened.

Her head dropped an inch, and she bared her teeth. A low, rumbling growl vibrated from her throat. She was warning me!

I gave her the thumbs up. "I'm ready."

With no clear idea of what awaited behind the doors, I held my hands in front of me, igniting my inner furnace. The time that had passed since I torched the woods outside had done the trick, there was no doubt in my mind. I could sense it. I was strong.

"Stand back," I whispered, and Jen obeyed. She took a position right next to me. "In three, two, one!"

With a surge so powerful I nearly fell backwards, I hurled a flame towards the doors. I tried to keep it in the shape of a cylinder, planning to blast the doors open so I could fire my glowing bullets at whoever was there. It seemed I had miscalculated the force.

The doors blew open, all right. They disintegrated the instant my flame-thrower hit them and didn't seem to slow the fire down the slightest. Five man-like torches behind the opening swayed and fell on the floor, which itself stood ablaze in a ten-foot-wide line towards the back wall. I pulled back, the flame no longer spurting from my palms. Jen's paws spun on the floor, leaving long trails from her claws in the dust as she jumped over the burning bodies. She landed and quickly jumped to the side to avoid getting burned on the hot part of the floor.

I followed, and for the first time since I discovered my firepower, I wondered if I could withstand fire altogether. I knew I didn't burn my hands when I let it out, but so far, I had never actually walked through fire, so to speak.

Instead of jumping over the burning corpses, I walked slowly between them. Flames licked my feet, but I didn't feel any pain. Looking down in awe, I soon realised what an idiot I was. My pants were not flame retardant at all, even if I seemed to be. Crouching, I patted the burning denim, thinking that I had to buy a new pair. I stomped my feet in an attempt to save what was left of my shoes. The soles had melted down to nothing more than a skin-like strip of rubber, or whatever soles were made of these days.

I quickly came out of the trance, though, as Jen's howl filled the hall. She was standing by the splintered door, the one Mordred had skewed with a piece of the guardrail. Crap! I had forgotten about that. The gangway was gone. It wouldn't be a problem for me, as I could always jump down to the floor below—maybe in a force field if I had to. Jen could definitely clear the opening. But we needed to find another way to get the Mags out of here.

I ran the few yards to Jen and peeked through the opening. Jen threw her head in front of me, pushing me back. A barrage of bullets hit the doorway, sending hundreds of tiny wooden shards flying everywhere. Dozens of them stung my skin like bees.

"How many?" I said, realising the absurdity of my question. "Never mind. I'll throw more fire at them." For some reason, it seemed that easy. Throw some fire, and burn the shit out of them. La de da!

The problem was that I had to stick at least parts of myself into the opening to do so, and while the bullets were on a break right now, the inferno was sure to ensue the millisecond I showed a fingertip.

"Any Jumpers here?" a thundering voice bellowed, crashing like a train through my gut.

Mordred!

There was no time to try and understand, though, as two guards popped up behind us out of thin air. Mum had told me about seeing a Magical like that before. She called him a Jumper.

Jen spun and bounced at the one closest to her. He hit her hard with a baseball bat. Jen whimpered and fell to the floor, blood coating the white fur on the side of her head.

"You bastard!" I screamed.

With a flick of my wrist, I sent a fireball—incidentally of about baseball size—towards him. It hit him in the chest but never stopped. He looked down at the gaping hole, then up at me, stupefied. I had no interest in exchanging glances.

Instead, I turned to the other guard, who came at

me with his own bat. In the back of my mind, a thought managed to flicker by. Jumpers couldn't bring metal with them on their jumps.

No gun then. Only a large piece of bonfire material.

In an instant, I set him ablaze. I wasn't even looking at him anymore. I didn't care. The rush inside me was as intoxicating as before, if not more wild, almost primal. These guys had tortured and killed Mags. My kind. No way would that happen again. I realised what I had to do to stop it. Who I had to get to.

Mordred.

The same anger that had encapsulated my thoughts when I suffocated Lionel filled me again.

Jen moaned and lifted her forepaws, trying to get to all fours. In the prison complex on the other side of the door, I heard footsteps. Boots on metal.

I slid over to Jen, placing my hand on her head. The difference between my fire and healing was black and white. I had to focus hard to switch this time, as my anger still burned inside. After a couple of seconds, the familiar light shone from my palm, and I pushed as much healing power into the wound as I could muster.

I had to let go sooner than I wanted, though it seemed to have worked well enough. At least Jen was on her feet and, by the look in her eyes, she was ready to fight.

"Come here!" Mordred thundered again, and for a second I thought he meant Jen and me.

I quickly understood what he was up to, however, when one guard after another came flying through the opening. Mordred was using his stolen magic to float—

or throw—them at us. One of the guards hit the side of what used to be a reinforced steel door frame, wrapping around it like a folding chair. His spine snapped with a crack as if it was a dry branch on a tree.

Mordred had succeeded in creating a frontal force, as the other four guards landed on the floor more or less unharmed. The first gun was already pointing at me, and soon we were surrounded.

There was no time to send fireballs at all of them. One or more of them would be able to hit Jen or me for sure.

I threw my hands outward, conjuring a massive force field. Not to encapsulate Jen and me, but to push the guards away. It worked. As the near-invisible dome hit them simultaneously, it threw them back in a semi-circle. The force field kept expanding. I made it expand. Breathing heavily, I pushed harder and harder, sliding the guards across the floor towards the walls. I let out a scream as I gave the dome a final push. All four of them were squeezed up against the wall, exploding like flies under a swatter. The force field and the walls were splattered with blood, guts, and bone fragments, like a grotesque modern art installation.

"Go to hell, you bastards!" I yelled.

"I'm sure they will," a voice said behind me.

I turned just in time to see Jen leap at Mordred, who didn't even flinch. He raised his left arm and knocked the big flying wolf straight back to where she had jumped from, sending her crashing to the floor. She skidded into the wall and slammed into it with a loud thump.

Mordred held his arms out. The walls started shaking like an earthquake hit the farm, and clouds of dust erupted as pieces of metal came flying out of the concrete. I threw a force field around myself, the rebar darts bouncing off it with tiny popping sounds.

The drugged-up policeman lowered his arms. "Time to end this charade, Ruby. You can't hide in that field forever, you know. At some point, your magic runs out, and then it's over. Why not save us both some time?"

"I'll kill you long before that." I clenched my jaw, not at all sure of myself.

"You won't, I'm afraid." His voice was calm, but the thunder was there, underneath the surface. "I've waited for this moment for a long time, Ruby Morgan. Or should I say Ruby Rivers?"

What the—?

He laughed. "I can tell by your expression that I'm right. Not that I had any doubt, of course. But where are my manners, good heavens? Brigham Jones at your service. Police superintendent, formerly known as Three. At least to your father."

"You—you knew my dad?"

"Briefly, yes. We were recruits at the Academy, for a few months."

I had no idea what he was on about. I did, however, have a strong idea about how long my force field would last. It tugged at me from the inside as my energy reached critically low levels. I had to hold on. Maybe Jen was ok. If I could hold on a couple of minutes more, she could get her bearings straight and sneak up on Mordred.

"You don't know! That's astonishing. What a terrible father, to keep such a thing from his own daughter."

"What are you talking about? What academy?"

"Only the first and best Harvester Academy ever. Dennis, or Seven as his recruit name was, showed such high promise. Came in from nowhere and made top of the class in no time. He was particularly apt at spotting Mags. Back then we had no scanners, you know. He made them on pure instinct. It was—pardon the pun —magic."

"Liar!" I spat the word at him. "Dad would never be one of you! Monsters and murderers, that's what you are, the lot of you. No way my dad—"

"When I kill you, Ruby Morgan Rivers, the last trace of that wanker is gone. Now, let that force field go, and throw those pathetic firecrackers at me, bitch!"

Darkness.

Not the kind I experienced in the van on the way up here.

This was inside me. It was black, rock-hard darkness. Pure anger.

I released it.

The answer to my worries about throwing fire from inside a force field was answered. Mordred's eyes widened, his face twisting in terror and surprise as the fireball blasted into his gut. He doubled over, clutching his belly. The thundering growl he had suppressed when talking surfaced again.

I had no power left to keep the force field up, and

he seemed to understand that. He lifted his trembling arm and flicked his hand. A three-foot-long piece of metal flew from the floor to my stomach. I stumbled but kept my footing. The blow was weak, revealing his fading powers.

"Your father was a coward, Ruby. Don't be one, too. Come here and fight me for real!"

"Fine by me." I moved slowly towards him.

He straightened his back, exposing his stomach and the large, burnt hole in his bulletproof vest.

"Oldest trick in the book," he sneered.

He held his arms out, like a satanic version of Jesus on the cross. Behind him, a rumbling began, and seconds later the wall came crashing down.

I threw myself to the floor as the iron spears flew over me and rammed into the far wall with tremendous force. So much for fading powers.

My breath came in short spurts, like at the end of a brutal interval run. Dots flashed before my eyes. Was there any fire left in me? If not, I was dead.

'You have immense powers, my dear Ruby. Immense.'

Hoping beyond hope that Gabriel's words rang true, I rolled over on my back and pointed at Mordred.

The room spun before my eyes as I let all my hatred and anger—all my darkness—flow out from the tip of my right index finger. A single blue flame erupted like a lightning bolt. It rushed at Mordred and hit his face, dead centre.

He had no time to react, and as the blue flame

turned into a red and orange inferno around him, he still stood with his arms spread out.

The now burning cross, which once had killed a beautiful, innocent Japanese girl, screamed. The guttural sound vibrated through the hall as the fire spread with it. I walked towards him, standing right in front of him.

I watched as the last ounce of life left his eyes, and his skin melted off his cranium. My heart played a drum solo in my heaving chest, and the heat was hellishly intense, but I didn't care. I wanted to see this. Needed to.

"Ruby!"

Way off in the distance, a voice called my name. Gabriel? Dad?

"Ruby, we have to get out of here! The whole place is burning!"

Jen!

I flinched out of my trance and turned to look for her. The room was full of smoke and flames. Jen sat in a corner, naked and human.

"Are you all right?" I shouted over the roar of the fire.

"Not really, but I will be. Had to shift to call for you!"

She closed her eyes, and I could see how much it cost her to shift back to her wolf shape. Still, the human Jen would have no chance of getting out of here.

The Mordred cross fell to the floor in a heap of ashen bones.

"Go!" I yelled.

Jen was already going, though not with her usual speed and grace. She had a terrible limp. Even so, she managed to run towards the far end of the burning hall, to the double doors and the corridor. I waited until she was out of sight, figuring she'd make it to the exit and across the field.

I turned and stepped over Mordred's remains. If there had been any guards left, they would have fired at me when I crouched through the opening, but nothing happened. One thought ran through my head.

Free them.

From the small remaining part of the gangway, I couldn't see the cages. I lowered myself as far as I could over the edge, and let myself drop to the floor ten feet below, softening the landing with a force field under my feet.

The chaos from my previous fireball escapades was even more devastating than I remembered. The fire had burned all flammable materials, leaving a soot-filled, concrete shell of a building. Tiny flames licked up one of the walls along with the minuscule remains of an electric wire.

Trying to preserve energy, I walked slowly past what had been my cage only hours ago. Minutes? Time was a floating concept. Everything had happened so fast, it was all a blur. The fatigue didn't exactly help either.

I found Oliver's cage, and sure enough, the keyring was still in the lock. I grabbed it and ran towards the stairs. Only one half of them remained, but I managed to climb them. At the top, I had to jump to reach the gangway towards the cages.

With all my focus on fighting off Mordred and his gang, making sure Jen was safe, and then finding the keys, I hadn't noticed the noise. A monotonous humming consisting of screams and moans filled the air and my ears. I had a premonition that my worst fears were about to be confirmed.

In the first eight cages, the prisoners lay slumped and lifeless, each with multiple gunshot wounds. In the ninth, an old man gripped the bars as I approached him.

"Please, help me! Help us, please!"

"I—I'll get you out. It's all right now." But how could I say those words when the guards must have strolled through here, from cage to cage, emptying their guns at the defenceless Magicals. Tears flowed as I searched for the right key. When I opened the cage, the old man with long silver hair threw his arms around me.

"Thank you! Thank you! They shot at us. Stabbed and hit us. I—I think they tried to get rid of—" His words drowned in his sobbing.

I wanted so badly to comfort him, but the screams and moans from the other cages called for me.

"They kept only the Pures and high-blooded," the man said, pulling away from me. "We need to save them. Let me help."

I couldn't believe my ears. How he didn't flee the scene was beyond me. He ran to the stairway and started to bend a piece of a metal bar back and forth. After a few repetitions, it gave in and broke off. No magic there, just knowledge.

I moved to the next cage, only to find another dead

person, a boy not more than fifteen. The old man started hitting the lock of another cage with the metal bar. Five clanking hits and the lock broke. He swung the door open to let a woman out.

"Stay close," I said to her. "We'll find a way out. All the guards are dead, so you're safe now, ma'am." I could be wrong, of course, but it seemed highly unlikely that any sentries were hiding somewhere now.

It took us between ten and fifteen minutes to free all the survivors of the massacre. Behind the last cage, where a man lay in a pool of blood, a door led to a back room. From there, the distance to another door was short. Behind it, the freezing morning air hit me, and I drew it in as deeply as I could.

We were at the back of the large barn, slash prison nightmare, atop a metal staircase.

"Stay here," I said to the motley crew of about twenty survivors and injured behind me. "It's too cold."

"We have to get away," cried a young woman. The left side of her face was crimson and slashed half-open, making her words come out in a slur. "They'll kill us all."

"They're gone," I said. "All of them. I'll get help. Stay inside, ok?"

It must have taken all their willpower to go back inside when freedom lurked just outside the door.

"I'll be back in a couple of minutes," I said. "Does anyone have any magic powers? I mean powers you can use right now?"

"They humanised all of us," the old man said. "Go. I'll stand guard by the door."

I ran out, my feet almost buckling from fatigue, but there was no way I would leave these Magicals alone for a second more than necessary. Turning the corner, I crossed the field to where I had left Oliver and Nick. Fifty yards. Forty. The black dots started dancing before my eyes again. Twenty.

A large figure appeared in a haze in front of me. Jen, in her soot-and-ashen covered white fur, stood guard in front of a bonfire with Oliver and Nick by her side.

Ten yards.

I fell flat on the ground at Jen's feet, registering somewhere way back in my mind that one of them was soaked in blood.

"Inside," I said, my voice dry and low. I tried clearing my throat.

"Ruby!" Nick ran towards me. "You're alive. Thank God. Are there any —?"

"They're inside, and they need our help," I said. "And protection."

# TWENTY

THE SMALL FIRES SURROUNDING ME CRACKLED WHILE I scooted closer to the flames. I shivered, my teeth chattering as I wrapped my arms around my knees. The stench of blood and gunpowder clogged my airways, sending me into a fit of coughs before a sharp pain careened up my spine. I gritted my teeth, unable to shed another tear.

I looked around. About twenty-odd people were huddled about a few scattered fires in what had been an open spaced living area, the kitchen still standing at one end. Most of the Mags sat or were curled up on the floor. I wanted to help them, but I was beat. I needed to refuel somehow. Weaving between the wounded, was Jen. She limped around the room on all fours, nudging people with her snout, continuing to sniff the openings in the walls, still alert and ready for any potential danger. The white of her fur was drenched in scarlet, and she kept her weight off one of her front paws. It was a stroke of luck that she had shown up when she did.

Beams from the morning sun penetrated the windows and charred openings in the wall, breaking into the puffs of ash that was heavy in the air, creating an eerie glow in the room. Gusts of chilling wind tore through the house. The remnants of the farmhouse provided shelter, but in my fiery frenzy, I had caused some sort of electrical meltdown, and there were no lights or heat apart from the sun outside, and some still burning planks.

A hand folded over my shoulder as Nick came to sit beside me.

"Still have that phone?" I asked.

The phone was already in his hand as he sat next to me. "Here."

I nodded at him and punched in the number I had memorised.

"Paddock," the man on the other end answered.

"It's Ruby."

"Son of a gun, Ruby. Where the heck are you?"

I sighed. Sounded like he had been looking for me. "Hertfordshire, I think. A farm called Warriner Fields. It's a MagX kind of farm." Or it used to be, I thought. "They caged me, but I'm all right now. There's a lot of dead people here, though, including a bunch of officers I assume came from your district. Can you please help?"

"Start at the beginning," he said grimly.

I told him the cliff-notes version, excluding the more horrible details.

For a long time, all I could hear was Paddock's deep breathing before he eventually found his words again.

"Listen, we've been looking for you since yesterday morning. Your friend, Charlie, rang me. I won't waste time with all the details, but let's just say she's discovered a lot. And so has Travers and the task force at Scotland Yard. You just sit tight. I'll make some calls, and it might take a little while, but I'll be there. Can you manage until then?"

"We'll have to, I suppose. Thanks, Paddock."

"Don't mention it. See you soon." He hung up.

I lifted my head to find Nick regarding me with his clear blue eyes. "I never knew you had it in you."

"What?"

"Your magic. I mean, you're a powerhouse, if I ever saw one. It's a little unnerving to watch in a sort of awe-inspiring scary kind of way."

I snorted and took in the sight of him. His red hoodie was in shreds. The crest with the once crossed hammers was barely recognisable where a shallow gash tore across his chest, and his arms were threaded with crimson wounds. Yet, his lips curved up.

"You want me to heal that for you?" I asked.

"Nah, I'll be ok. Besides, the scars will make me look badass, and I think you should save your energy for those who really need it."

For a human, Nick had stood his ground, fighting as ferociously as the rest of us. It was more than a little impressive.

"So," I said. "How exactly did you escape to find me?"

"An illusionist never reveals his tricks." He winked. "Sleight of hand. Let's just say that I've practised slipping out of ropes before. Not that hard once you know what to do. Besides, I don't think those officers that bound me were especially familiar with tying people up."

I blinked, trying to process what he had said. "Wait, back up. Illusionist?"

He grunted. "Well, yeah. My gramps used to pull pennies from my ear and extract random things out from his sleeves. So, ever since I was a kid, I wanted to be able to perform magic, which, since I'm not a natural-born Mag—" He glanced at me. "I had to find other ways. When my gramps died, he left me a book on illusions with all sorts of neat tricks in it. I suppose it's the closest thing to actual magic I'll get, save from licking MagX."

I scowled at him, and he waved his hands defensively.

"Which I am never going to do again! I promise. This was a serious wake-up call. I can't believe this is what it takes to get MagX into the hands of users. It hadn't occurred to me."

I mused, happy Nick had come around, yet something was nagging at me. "I think," I said, "I think this is just the tip of a giant iceberg. This was organised like there was a chain of command and someone outside with higher authority, cash changing hands. Who knows how far up the chain goes? We haven't seen the half of it, I think."

"Now, that's a chilling thought."

I nodded, brushing the thought away for later. "Then what? I mean, what happened next with your escape?"

He shrugged. "Once I wiggled my way out of the ropes, the rest was pure adrenalin—panic and anger. I knew I had to find you. So, I got a hold of a metal rod and swung it like a supercharged Sir Ian Botham on MagX."

I had no idea who this Botham-bloke was, but knowing Nick, he was probably some sort of sports hero.

"Got room?" Jen asked, taking a seat next to me. She was back in her human form, naked as a baby, showing bloodied teeth in a wide grin.

"Always." I didn't care that she was naked, or about the jolts of pain coursing through me as I swung my arms around her. "I'm so, so happy you came."

"So am I, pup," Jen cooed.

Nick cleared his throat, and I sat back to look at him. His gaze wavered, shifting every which way, and underneath all the grit on his cheeks, I could swear they were turning a rosy pink.

"Should maybe find you some clothes," he mumbled, scrambling off outside.

I laughed. It hurt, but it was good to laugh.

Nick returned shortly after with a pair of sweat-pants and a black t-shirt. "The best I could do. Might be some blood on it, though. He angled his head away from Jen as she accepted the clothes and proceeded to slip into them.

"Thanks," she said. "You're free to look now."

After a few seconds of hesitation, Nick sat back beside her. "Nice of you to join us."

"And not a moment too soon. I tried tracking you all day. Took a train yesterday morning, and have been running around farms ever since. Might have scared a sheep or ten. We knew you were likely somewhere in Hertfordshire or nearby, but it's been a real bitch to catch your scent. Not like we had a lot to go on. But then, tonight, it was there—plus, the raging fire was a dead giveaway. I trailed you through the woods, and found you in this mess."

I bit the insides of my cheeks. It had been a close call. If Jen hadn't shown up when she did, I would probably be dead. And if Nick hadn't saved me before I was injected with more human blood, we wouldn't have escaped at all.

"Thank you for saving my ass," I said firmly.

Jen nodded.

"Both of you," I added.

Nick shrugged. "Team effort."

Jen's already arched eyebrows rose as she regarded Nick with bright eyes before shifting closer to him. "Guess I owe you thanks as well, for saving my girl."

Nick flashed a grin, his battered chest rising, and I briefly worried that his wound would deepen by the motion, but he didn't seem to notice it as his attention was strictly for Jen.

I left them by the fire to check on the other Mags. They ranged in age. I remembered seeing the youngest boy in one of the cages, so small and terrified. He wasn't badly hurt, however, and Oliver kept him entertained with some story that made the boy giggle. Most likely, Oliver was boasting about himself, so I passed by them to the old man who sat in a corner, his back resting against the wall.

Silver hair trailed backwards from his forehead, running all the way down to his waistline. His chest rose in shallow breaths, hairline gashes crisscrossing across his forearms, and blood seeping from his stomach.

I rushed over and knelt by his side. "It's all right," I mumbled. "I'll help you."

His eyelids parted slightly and his amber eyes, faceted with green specks, peered out at me. He gave a tilt of his chin before his eyelids drooped again.

Taking a deep breath, I summoned back the warmth nestling in my veins. It was weak, but it was there. I placed my hands over the man's stomach, and a dim light shone underneath my palms. Beads of perspiration coated my forehead as I maintained the magic for as long as I could. The blood finally stopped flowing, and the wound closed enough to contain it. No longer able to keep it up if I needed it again for anyone else, I willed the magic back inside. He wasn't completely healed, but he wasn't dying at the moment either. It would have to be enough for now.

"Car," Jen called, her ears pricking up.

I sprinted for the door as fast as my body would allow, and opened it halfway, shielding my body as I looked outside. It was too soon to be Paddock.

A Volkswagen Transporter pulled up outside. I

readied myself for whatever was to come, sucking air into my lungs. The passenger door opened.

And out stepped Charlie.

My heart bounced. I flung the door wide open and darted forwards, pain be damned. We met in an embrace. She sobbed into my hair, and my tears crept back as well. Only this time, they were tears of joy. Charlie was here. I didn't want to let go, but we couldn't stay like that forever. Reluctantly, I stepped out of the embrace and met her gaze.

Her jaw dropped. "Holy cow, Ru!"

"I know." Gently, I wiped a tear from her cheek.

"I wish I had found you sooner."

"It's all right. You're here now. Come to think of it, how are you here? Jen call you?"

"Nah, she's been wolfing it out. I've spent the time since your disappearance looking at satellite images, trying to find your dang weathervane somewhere in the fudging haystack. I narrowed it down to three farms— you really ought to take an art class—then matched the name to the letters you gave me."

"You brilliant little digiwizard," I said.

Another car door opened and shut, and Duncan strolled towards us.

"Duncan! You're out!" I gave him a hug, and he hugged me back.

"Heard you were in trouble." He slid his fingers through his hair. It was clean for a change, soft and shiny. Everything about him was sleeker than I remembered. Rehab must have been good for him. "I just—" He spun slowly, his face shifting out towards the scene of the recent fight. "This is mad. I can't believe my stupidity."

I squeezed his hand for reassurance. "You're clean now, though, right?"

"As a whistle."

The purr of an engine sounded somewhere by the main road before another car came up the driveway. I stiffened, slipping straight back into fight mode.

"Easy," Charlie said. "I rang him."

Brendan!

The car parked next to the Volkswagen, and Brendan stepped outside.

I froze at the sight of him, my emotions wild and shifting inside. He locked eyes with me, those stunning, breath-taking eyes. The breeze ruffled his hair as he sped up and ran towards me.

Warmth. Safety. The spicy smell of his aftershave. It was all-consuming as his arms slid around my waist, his hands carefully caressing the bare skin underneath my shirt at the small of my back.

"I was so scared," he breathed.

I buried my head in the nape of his neck, inhaling the scent of him, feeling his warmth spread through me. My fingers laced in his hair while his hands moved over my hips, then back up to my waist. His grip was firm, yet gentle. The world around us disappeared for a moment. All my hurt and anger seeped away from me, and all I felt was a burning desire, hope, and something else, something strong and glorious that made my heart expand in my chest, my breath slowing steadily before his lips grazed my collar bone, sending sweet shivers through my body and my pulse rising.

I lifted my head to face him, his breath an invitation on my lips. I closed my eyes and leaned into him, his heart beating steadily along with my own.

"Is he here?" someone said, ripping me out of my euphoria.

Brendan's arms slipped away from me as Teagan pushed him aside and took his place.

I blinked and licked my lips. My unkissed-by-Brendan lips.

"Well?" she asked, her hands on her hips.

I nodded.

"Teagan!" Oliver swooped past me to scoop Teagan up and into his arms. I jumped back to avoid Teagan's dangling feet kicking me in the chest. He put her down and kissed her with raw, unabashed passion, making my cheeks flush.

I glanced at Brendan, who held his palms out to me and shrugged. Our moment had passed, and I became suddenly aware of how I had to look—not to mention smell.

Oliver unlinked himself from Teagan to look at me. "They need you inside, Ru. There's a woman in there, Ivy, in dire need of healing. We don't have time to wait for an ambulance."

Brendan stared at me and his brows deepened, confusion written in the way his expression shifted. No time to worry about that, though, so I took a deep breath and hurried back inside.

The woman, whom I expected was Ivy, lay in the

centre of the room. Her black-as-night locks were braided in a hundred small braids, fanning out around her head. Her skin would have been a rich brown, I thought, though it carried a greyish tint. Her eyes were open but vacant.

"Any other Fae in this room with healing power?" I called. I was exhausted, and my powers had just run a marathon.

Heads shook all around.

I sighed and knelt beside Ivy. "Hey," I said. "I'm Ruby."

Her auburn eyes caught my gaze swiftly to reveal a hint of awareness. There was still time if only I could summon enough power to help her.

"I don't see any wounds." There were plenty of bruises but no open wounds. I had no idea where to focus my energy.

"She took a pretty heavy hit," Oliver said as he and the entourage from outside joined me by the woman. Brendan was there as well, though he kept his distance, standing in the shadows beside a window, light streaming past but not on him.

"Right," I muttered, shaking my head.

"I think her rib cage took the worst blow. Internal bleeding would be my best guess," Oliver offered.

It was the best I had to go on, so I leaned forward, one hand above Ivy's heart, the other on her forehead.

Nothing happened. I was drained and hurt and simply miserable.

Charlie crouched opposite me, handing me a bottle

of water. "You are the most amazing person I know. If anyone can find the strength, you can."

I smiled weakly and swigged the water down. If Charlie had this much faith in me, I should too. Again, I reached for my magic, for the calm centre of my being. There had been so much death, and my anger and fury still lingered in my veins. Pushing through the hate, the remorse, my sadness and my fear, I found one last strand of light. The sensation of serenity and hope, of happiness and love. I focused on it, picturing the sliver of warmth in my mind. A blast of light erupted from my palms, briefly illuminating the entire room before surging back, the light folding over Ivy, rays of healing spilling under her skin.

Ivy held my gaze then, her eyes growing alert and wise. The hint of a smile spread out, and I released the magic, feeling it flow back to rest in my blood once more.

"That was a rush." Ivy rose by the flat of her hands. "Thank you."

I nodded at her, quickly surveying the wide eyes and the other injured all around, then stood and strode back outside. The weight of everyone weighed heavily on my shoulders. I had managed to draw on a last hair of energy, but that was all I had left to offer. I could sense it as I stood there in the middle of the evidence of the carnage I had wrought. I let out an exasperated breath.

This was my doing. Sure, the 'Sentries of Camelot' played their part, but I could have found other ways. I could have locked them inside force fields and given them a bump on the head before tying them up. Yet I had chosen fire and destruction every step of the way. How many had I killed last night? I hardly recognised who I was anymore. Not only that, but according to Mordred, my life was a lie. Dad had been a Harvester, and if he had been here last night, I would have surely torched him along with all the others.

A tear swam from my eye. I would get the answers I needed one way or the other. First, though, I had to help the injured Mags, and I knew exactly who to call, even if I didn't want to. I couldn't wait around for Paddock and his task force. That would place the Mags here on record, listed as Magicals for anyone to know, which meant public hospitals were not an option. They needed care, however, and I had nothing left to give. Certainly not to that many people.

I inhaled sharply and rang Mum.

# TWENTY-ONE

I RESTED MY HEAD AGAINST THE PASSENGER WINDOW AS the Volkswagen sped north. The hum of the engine was a constant reminder that we were getting closer by the minute. I only hoped it wouldn't be too late to save everyone. We had filled the two cars with as many as we could. Unsurprisingly, Oliver had a way with cars, and when the smaller cars were both full, he had hotwired one of the vans on the farm. It was a chore to fit everyone inside, but we made it work. He had taken charge of his own car after that, and Brendan had volunteered to drive the van after there was no longer room for me to go with him. He hadn't said a word to me after I healed Ivy, and maybe he never would again.

Charlie stretched forward from the back seat and put a hand over mine. "Don't worry, babe. He'll come around."

I hadn't breathed a word about Brendan out loud, yet somehow, Charlie just knew. She didn't have an issue with Jen or me being Mags, perhaps Brendan would understand in his own time? I had my doubts.

I sagged against the door and forced myself to think about something other than Brendan. We were only about an hour away from Mum's clinic, and though I had not seen her for weeks, I wasn't looking forward to the talk we were bound to have. I had lied to her, kept things from her, and she would know that now. Then again, if Dad had been a Harvester, she had to have known. And if she did know, then what else was she lying about? Up until now, I had been so sure that Dad's MagX overdose wasn't his fault, that he was somehow forced to take it or given it by accident. After watching how the officers all helped themselves to the drug, I was no longer certain. Maybe he just wasn't the man I thought he was.

"Professor Kaine asked for you, by the way," Charlie said.

"He did?"

"Uhuh, he came by our flat yesterday. Said something about trying to contact you for some sort of private tutoring or something. The professor seemed really worried about you."

I hadn't even thought about that. I was supposed to meet him for another training session in the boiler room yesterday morning. "I'll have to text him."

"Already done. I told him you were safe and sound, taking a few days at your mum's place. What is he tutoring you for anyway?"

"It's—I'll tell you later." The phone buzzed in my pocket, and I answered the call.

"It's Paddock. Got your text about leaving the farm. You neglected to tell me you left with all the bodies, too."

"Huh? What are you talking about?" I asked, sitting up straight.

"I mean there's nothing here, no people or bodies at all. We've just arrived, Travers and his men too. They're sweeping the area, but besides a burnt down farm and a lot of scorched earth, there are no signs that there was ever anything but a farm here."

I shook my head in disbelief. How long since we left? Not long at all. And someone had already wiped out all the evidence? I shuddered at the thought.

"I swear, I'm telling the truth," I said.

"I believe you. In fact, I'm kind of glad we don't have a ton of police officers' bodies to deal with, though we're bound to get a bunch of missing persons reports. Your friend Charlie has been a great help, though. The money trail is enough to establish corruption, and the chat room for Sentries of Camelot, well, Charlie's been a tremendous help cracking the code names there as well. The things they've shared in that chat room alone should be enough to shut down this group for good."

"Really?" That was great news. Though I might have shut down a good chunk of the so-called Sentries of Camelot myself, there would surely be more of them than those guarding the farm.

"Don't go getting too excited, though," Paddock said. "Someone was feeding them money and giving them instructions, but not even the Yard has been able to crack the source. In either case, Sentries of Camelot is history. Travers has some big names on his list. I'd watch the news for the next couple of days if I were you."

"Thanks. I appreciate it." Tip of a very large iceberg, I thought.

"Tell Charlie to stop poking around the police network from now on though, all right."

I smirked at the phone. "Will do." Another thought occurred to me then. "By the way, how is that skater boy doing? Is he safe?"

"No worries. The boy is perfectly safe and sound. I thought about what you said about him needing protection, and Travis has taken him into a witness protection program. Turns out that the skaters were all Mags, and Fernsby had been on their tail for a while. The bandana I found, the girl he killed before our trip to the skatepark—they were all part of the same crew."

The pieces clicked together in my head, and I sighed with relief. "I appreciate everything you've done. Thank you!"

"Don't mention it."

He ended the call, and I slumped back in the seat again.

Duncan turned the volume up on the radio, and Ozzy Osbourne told us he was a dreamer. Charlie tuned in, bellowing the lyrics behind me. Duncan winced and shook his head before he changed the channel, leaving us with "Moves Like Jagger" instead.

"Thanks for coming to help," I told him.

"My program was done last week. I had planned to take a couple of weeks somewhere to just relax, but when Charlie said she needed a car, and that someone had kidnapped you and Nick, what else was I supposed to do?"

I smiled at him. He had come a long way since I first met him back in Craydon. The constant jitter of his hands was nowhere to be seen, and he looked content —happy even. At least some of us were. I had a hard time letting go of my grim mood. We had stopped to fill gas and grab a quick bite, which helped, but my body was aching all over the place. I was stiff and sore, and no matter how I shifted my weight on the seat, my back complained, my arm hurt, my head hurt. Everything just hurt.

I could ask Mum to heal me, but that would be selfish. There were a lot of Mags much worse for wear than me coming with us to the clinic. She would have her hands full, and I didn't want to get in her way or risk a confrontation yet. She had been so distant on the phone once I started telling her about where I was, and how I got there. I omitted to tell her that I had killed people or that I had used my recently discovered firepower to do so. Although, she would probably put two and two together on her own. When I told her about the injured Mags, however, Mum didn't hesitate. She told me to get moving and bring everyone to her as quickly as possible.

So, here we were, headed towards Mum's clinic with a heap of injured Magicals and a heck of a story to tell.

We pulled up to the back delivery entrance of the clinic as Mum had instructed.

A man in a white coat waved at us from outside the steel doors. I'd met him a few times before when visiting the clinic with Mum, and he had that kind of look you never forget. Wisps of stringy, white strands were all that could be said to pose as hair on his head. He had ears that would make Dumbo proud, and a long beak-like nose set under wise and beady eyes. The furrows on his skin portrayed roadmaps for a life long-lived, yet he appeared exactly the same to me as the first time I remembered seeing him all of fifteen years back. He had known me prior to what I could recall from memory, though, as he was there the day I was born.

"Hi, Hugo," I said as I popped the door closed behind me.

He tilted his chin at me. "Lots of folks you're bringing, Ruby."

"There's twenty-seven of us, though not all of us need instant care. We have seven with gunshot wounds, five with other severe injuries, and the rest are minor, though most of them could use a full check-up."

"I see."

I looked past him into the corridor beyond, which was more like looking over him. Hugo was short, as if he had stopped growing at the age of ten. "Where's Mum?"

"Elaine's here. She went to prep the rooms. The clinic isn't really equipped to deal with this amount of special guests."

"Thank you. We'll need gurneys."

"You got some able bodies in those cars? I have five gurneys inside, though not a lot of staff to manage them. Bring in the ones who need it the most first, then return for the others."

"Right on it," I said.

I continued to instruct Duncan, Nick, Jen, then reluctantly Brendan, taking charge of the fifth gurney myself.

"I'll help you with that," Charlie said.

We proceeded to get those with gunshot wounds onto the gurneys, and pushed them inside, following at Hugo's heels. He turned a corner, then pressed the button for the lift.

I cleared my throat. "The ER is on this floor."

"I should know," Hugo said.

"Are you going to get Mum? Should we continue to the ER alone?"

"No, child. We are going downstairs."

There was no downstairs. This was ground level, and there were only two floors above us. Had the old man finally lost his marbles?

"You really shouldn't gawk like that. It's not becoming of someone such as yourself," Hugo said.

The doors gave a ding, and Charlie and I pushed the first gurney inside. Duncan followed, then Nick. There wasn't enough room for the last two gurneys, however, and Hugo made the rest wait by the door for his return.

I narrowed my eyes at the buttons. Had Hugo meant up when he said down?

Instead of pushing any button at all, Hugo reached into one of the large pockets on his coat and fished out a key. He inserted it into the keyhole underneath the panel of buttons and turned it until it gave a click.

"Why down?" I asked.

"Can't very well have all these Magicals in the regular ER. I'm sure you understand the need for discretion."

Shortly thereafter the lift moved and the doors opened back up.

"No time to dawdle," Hugo said, hastening out of the lift and into a wide corridor. We pushed the gurneys after him as I surveyed the space. There were no windows, just a long, empty corridor with a few doors on either side. The walls looked thick, as if they were reinforced with some material I didn't recognise. In fact, I didn't recognise this place at all. Downstairs. Hugo hadn't lost any marbles—there really was a downstairs. One I had never been privy to. Another deception.

"In here." Hugo pressed a switch on the wall and a set of double doors opened for us. The room was spacious; enough for all five gurneys along with a range of medical equipment, monitors, and cabinets covering the back wall. In the centre of the room, by a large desk, sat Mum.

"Right, I'll leave you to it and go fetch the others." Hugo walked back out and down the corridor again.

Mum looked up at me from the microscope she had been staring into. Her gaze moved up and down, and her smooth forehead wrinkled into a slight frown. A few strands of strawberry-blonde hair stuck out underneath her head cover. She stood and walked up to the closest gurney, the one Nick was in charge of.

"Status?" she asked.

"Gunshots. Three of them. Critical, I think," Nick said.

"And the others?"

"About the same."

Mum sighed, then came up to me. She gave me a quick hug, void of the usual warmth she carried. "Can you heal?"

"Hi, Mum." A sense of annoyance crept over my skin. "I'm fine thanks. I've done as much healing as I could manage, however, and I don't have much more left in me right now."

She stroked a hand over my hair and shook her head. "Then you should go home. Take your friends who are not in dire need of medical attention and come back in the morning. The rest of the Magicals can stay in the rooms we've got here."

"What is this place?" I asked.

"Later," Mum said. "I need to help these people now. I promise we'll talk later."

Another doctor and a nurse entered the room, and the three of them busied themselves with tending to the new arrivals.

"I guess we go home then," I said.

Charlie grinned. "Sleepover at the Morgans'."

"It's a small house. I'm not sure if we can fit everyone in."

Jen wrapped her arm over Charlie's shoulder and shrugged. "I'm fine with the floor."

"All right, then Charlie can sleep in my bed with me. Duncan can get the sofa."

"My bed is available," Mum called, her hands glowing brightly as she moved them over one of the injured Mags. Whoever the other staff were, they knew what she was. Were they Mags, too?

"Sweet. I'll get Mummy Morgan's bed then," Nick said, a little too much enthusiasm in his voice, and a low growl sounded from Jen's throat.

"That leaves Brendan, Oliver and Teagan." As I said it, the three of them came through the doors. There really was no need for Teagan as she was clinging to Oliver like a bee to honey, clearly not helping with the gurney at all.

"What are we doing?" Oliver asked.

"Leaving." Inhaling sharply, I forced myself to meet Brendan's eyes. He averted his gaze and moved closer to the door.

"Sleepover at the Morgans'," Charlie quipped. "I have dreamt of this."

"I actually think we should head back to London," Brendan muttered. "I have a fencing class tomorrow, and I don't need any treatment. Neither does Teagan." He still wasn't looking at me when he spoke, his face lowered as if he was inspecting his shoes.

"I'm cool with driving back tonight," Oliver said. "There's nothing wrong with me that a few days' rest won't fix." His arm slid around Teagan's waist as he said 'rest'.

I was about to argue when Hugo lumbered inside. "You're crowding the room. Get the rest of the injured inside, and leave. Nothing more you can do here. I've prepared food and drinks for the lot of them. I promise, they would not get better treatment anywhere else."

Too tired to start arguing with anyone, I conceded. I made an attempt to wave at Mum, but she had moved on to her next patient, even though her first patient was far from fully healed. She was saving energy, distributing it as best she could to make sure she kept everyone alive. It was something I needed to learn.

At least the Mags were in good hands, and as Hugo had pointed out, there was nothing more for us to do here. Besides, my stomach was growling like Jen's wolf, and I was about to fall asleep on my feet. Charlie and Jen linked their arms in mine, and we walked out.

Teagan and Ollie got back in his car, and Brendan promised to dump the van near the farm on the way back before catching a ride to campus with the others.

The rest of us, Charlie, Jen, Nick, Duncan and myself, drove towards the little brick house—home.

On the way there, we stopped at my favourite pizza place, buying one pizza for each person, two for Jen.

We huddled together in the small living area, and I ate like I hadn't had food for weeks. The room looked exactly the way it had when I left for uni, apart from the cat bed beside a scratching post next to the sofa.

A soft purr caught my attention as Kit strutted in from the kitchen. He stopped suddenly, his hairs on end, and hissed. Jen narrowed her eyes at him, her lip folding away from her teeth. The staring contest ended with Kit taking a detour across the room and behind the sofa to jump into my lap.

"Hey, Kit." I scratched him behind his ears. He had grown.

"Gawd, this is a class A pizza, Ru!" Charlie licked her lips, aiming for another slice.

"Right!" And it had never tasted as good as it did at that moment.

Duncan turned the telly on, and it was somehow comforting how normal it felt.

"So, I want a full account," Charlie said.

I wanted to tell her everything, while at the same time, I was afraid of what she would think of me.

"Ruby is like an effing goddess," Nick said. "You should have seen her! Fire and wrath. Total sock-knocking experience. And Jen's wolf! Just wow! I had no idea you guys were packing this kind of mojo, or I would definitely have kept my gob shut."

Jen rolled her eyes at him, though the corner of her lips quirked up. "*Hashtag Girlpower.*"

"Sorry, Jen, this does not end up on your Insta." I wasn't really worried. Jen posted all sorts of pictures to her Insta, all of which were made to fit her feminism profile, but she had more common sense than most people. I didn't have to tell her to keep our recent escapades under wraps.

"Hey, turn the sound up," Nick said.

Every one of us gaped at the screen.

*"—being brought to the waiting police cars. We're speaking to Inspector Nigel Travers of Scotland*

262

Yard. Inspector Travers, what can you tell us about today's operation?" The reporter held a microphone towards the uniformed policeman.

"Not much at the moment, I'm afraid. The situation is ongoing. What I can say is that several high-level officers in the Metropolitan Police have been brought in for questioning."

"There are rumours of corruption, Inspector."

"No comments at this stage."

The clip in the background showed several men being escorted out of the Richmond Police Station, some in uniforms and some in black suits. The press, with shouting journalists and flashing cameras, surrounded the men and the cars. What chaos.

The reporter turned towards the camera. "Back to you in the studio, Jon."

"Thank you, Steve."

The anchor cleared his throat and turned to a woman on his left. "And just arriving in our studio is Gwendolyn Sparks, spokeswoman for the Ministry of Justice. What can you tell us about this shocking situation?"

"Well, Jon, as our Secretary of State for Justice, the

*Right Honourable Martin Cheeves, promised four years ago, we have put measures in place to handle these matters."* Jon, the anchor, leaned forward.

*"And what matters are we talking about?"*

*"I cannot go into details about the composition of the ... let's call it a task force for now. They have gathered huge amounts of evidence over the past months, and today we see the results of their excellent work. A group of police officers, ranking from the lowest PC to the highest levels at the police station in question—"*

*"That's Richmond Station, right?"*

The woman held her hand up to wave him off. *"As I said, the station in question. This group of police officers have operated outside the scope of the law, and Scotland Yard has, therefore, intervened on behalf of the Crown and the citizens of London. And our country."*

*"They call themselves 'Sentries of Camelot', we've learned during the last hours."*

*"So we've heard, yes. Apparently, they've used code-names to stay hidden."*

*"Knights' names, right?"*

*"Yes, so it seems. But instead of dwelling on such nonsense, I would like to point out what an excellent job our protectors at Scotland Yard have done. We are talking day and night surveillance, months of meticulous research across several branches of the force, including undercover work on the dark web, and—"*

*"They seem to have used secret chat rooms,"* Jon said. *"On the dark web. How were they spotted?"*

*"That would be too risky for me to go into details on, Jon. Suffice to say that our friends at Scotland Yard have some of the best cyber-investigators on the face of the planet."*

"Turn it off." Charlie stretched her arms behind her head. "Let them gloat. We all know who the real cyber-investigator is, right?"

She grinned at me, and I couldn't help grinning right back at her.

# TWENTY-TWO

CHARLIE'S SNORES WERE COMFORTING AFTER THE TIME I had spent at the farm. I tossed and turned through the night, however, and as the first hint of light crept over the windowsill, I got up.

I pulled on a pair of my old sweats and struggled to lift my arms to get the t-shirt on before I slipped into my furry tiger slippers, and stepped down the stairs with Kit bouncing lightly by my feet.

"Stay close," Jen whispered from where she lay curled up on a sheepskin by the fireplace.

"Just going outside for a bit," I whispered back.

She stretched and turned to curl up again as I walked out onto the back patio. The grass was frosted, and it glittered in the dawn. I shivered a little from the cold but didn't want to disturb anyone by going back inside to get a jacket. Instead, I sat down on the garden swing, facing the pond and the trees beyond. The last time I had sat by the pond felt like forever ago, almost like a dream. Mum and I had performed a ritual before

I left for university, and we had written down three wishes each, offering them to the Lady of the Lake. I hadn't thought much about my wishes since.

*What had I wished for?*

Friends had been my first wish, I recalled. True friends with whom I could share everything. Had that wish not come true? I had real friends in Charlie and Jen, loyal and caring friends. Duncan had shown up when he learned I was in trouble, and he knew what I was as well. Even Nick was becoming a closer friend than I could have imagined. He could've run when he freed himself, yet he went looking for me and saved my life. Although Brendan was mad at me, or whatever he was, my first wish had come true. As for my second wish, I had wished for Mum to find purpose with me gone, so that she wouldn't be lonely. Was that what she was doing at the clinic? Finding her purpose?

My third wish, however, was something I had yet to see granted, and probably never would. But it didn't matter. I would work on that one later. I should be happy I was granted one wish, and maybe even two of them. Mum had been so sure that the Lady had heard us, and maybe she had. I crossed my legs on the swing and pulled my arms into my sleeves as the coughs of the old Ford Fiesta issued from the gravel road on the other side of the house. The engine noise cut off before the door popped shut and footsteps followed.

Mum came around the corner of the house as if she had known I was there.

"Morning, love," she said, taking a seat next to me. "Got you a blanket and green tea with a splash of lemon for the both of us." She placed the blanket around my shoulders and gave me a disposable cup from a cup holder, making me insert my arms into the holes on the t-shirt again.

"How did you know I was back here?" I asked.

"Darling, you always come here when you're broody."

I hadn't given it much thought before, though now that she mentioned it, I realised she was right. This had always felt like a safe zone, a good quiet place to think.

I looked at Mum from the corner of my vision. The fine wrinkles around her eyes had deepened since I left home, and there was a sort of drawn expression on her face. She sighed and leaned back on the swing, giving it a light push that made it sway gently back and forth.

I took a sip of my tea, the warmth spreading through me like a shield against the cold. "How are the Mags doing?"

Mum pulled her feet onto the swing. "We lost one of the young girls." A tear ran down Mum's cheek. "She had internal bleeding. We didn't catch it in time, and when we did, I had no more healing power in me to save her."

I drew in a breath, the cold air surging back into me.

"The rest are in recovery." Mum wiped her cheek. "They'll all recover in time."

The tea was already lukewarm as I took another sip. "What was that place, Mum?"

She sniffled, inhaling deeply. "We have seen an increasing amount of Mags coming through the clinic these past few years, and the hospitals are noticing as well. All information goes on record, making the Magicals vulnerable, not to mention easy pickings for any Harvester. But you know that. It's why I always healed your wounds and major illnesses, instead of taking you to the hospital when you were little. So, over the past few years, Hugo, his wife, and I have worked to create a place where we can treat Magicals off the record. It's not much, and it doesn't have the required room for what we want to be able to provide, but it's a start."

Purpose, I thought. My second wish was, if not fulfilled, then certainly on its way.

"So, spill. Your turn," Mum said. "It's time for you to talk. You only told me what I had to know on the phone. Now, I want you to tell me everything."

I took a deep breath and told Mum almost everything. I told her about the almost kidnapping back in September, about the Harvester following me. I told her about the Sentries of Camelot, about the visions I had been having, and about how Nick and I were captured.

"And how exactly did you manage to escape?" Mum gave me a stern look, as if she knew I was holding back.

I was on a roll, so I might as well get more than my feet wet.

"Fire," I said, biting my lip. "It's not just the visions. Lately, I've been able to summon fire."

Mum gave an audible gasp, and her cup dropped to the ground, the rest of her tea flowing over the edge of the patio and onto the grass.

I twirled my ring around my finger and closed my

eyes for a moment. "I never had it before, then one day it was there. But it can't just appear like that, can it?"

Mum shook her head but made no further comment, so I continued the recount of my escape from the farm, omitting the gory details. She didn't need to know about my sudden desire to kill the men who had caged me.

"I should have never allowed you to leave," Mum said. "It was foolish of me, but you should have told me sooner, Ruby. I wish you'd been honest with me."

"You mean like you've been honest with me?" My tone was clipped, and the burst of anger that had started to become so familiar flared back to life.

"Ruby Guinevere Morgan. That is no way to talk to your mum!"

"You've been lying to me all my life. How should I respond?"

A small flame erupted from my palm, lighting the cup on fire. I dropped it, and it rolled to support itself against Mum's cup as the flames died down.

"I don't—" She averted her face, her lips quivering. "I'm not sure what you mean."

"I'm talking about Dad. How you never told me the truth about who he was."

She stared at me then, her eyes wide, and something else. She looked terrified. She opened and shut her mouth, but no words came out, so I took that as my cue to keep talking.

"Why did you never tell me Dad was a Harvester?"

"A Harvester? Lady Lake, who told you that?"

"One of the men at the farm, Mordred. Said he went by Five, and that he knew Dad as Seven."

Mum took my hands, and I flinched at her touch. She withdrew, twining her fingers in her lap instead. "Yes, Ruby. Dad was Seven—for a while. Until he wasn't."

I had known it was true, somewhere inside I had known. To hear it from Mum's lips, however, was an entirely different experience. She had just confirmed Mordred's words.

"You have to understand, it was different then. Your dad was so young, and much like you, he lost his own father at the hands of the MagX industry. He blamed Mags for his father's death, which is why he went out of his way to join the Academy."

"The Academy?"

"The Harvester Academy. The MagX industry is a massive operation, love. But your dad, he didn't have all the facts, and he was nothing like the men who kidnapped you. Dennis never knew about the farms before he learned about them at the Academy. He was a good man, and he loved you, with or without your gifts."

"I can't believe it," I cried. "Dad was ... and you didn't tell me. You say Dad never had the facts, but you have always warned me about Harvesters, and yet you never told me the entire truth either."

Her gaze fell. "There is, there's much for us to talk about. I guess I didn't want you to think ill of him. He was the dad you remember, darling, even if—" She shook her head and shut her eyes hard, a stream of tears trapped between her eyelids.

"Even if what?" I pressed.

"Nothing, I—it's not important. We have both had our fair share of revelations." She opened her eyes again and stared at me with warm, tired eyes. "I'm sorry you feel deceived, and I understand that you are an adult now and that you don't have to tell me everything. But, honey, when it comes to your powers, and dangerous situations like those you've found yourself in lately, I hope you can find it in you to trust me with it."

Mum stood. She patted my knee and walked into the house, leaving me alone on the swing again.

I stared defiantly at the tree line when a movement caught my eye. A dark mist rose between the trunks and slivers of inky shades drifted out from within. An ominous shape of a man appeared like a mirage of smoke and shadows from the mist. It was my old shadowy friend. Mum had said she would tell me what she knew about it, though with everything that had happened, it didn't seem like the right time to press her for answers. Still, I couldn't help but wonder. It occurred to me that I hadn't seen him for a while. And now, there he was, as if he was checking up on me. I waved at the shadowy form and wrapped the blanket tight around me. I had changed. I could feel it lurking inside like the shadow staring at me from the darkness.

# BOOK THREE

## VIRTUES OF PURITY

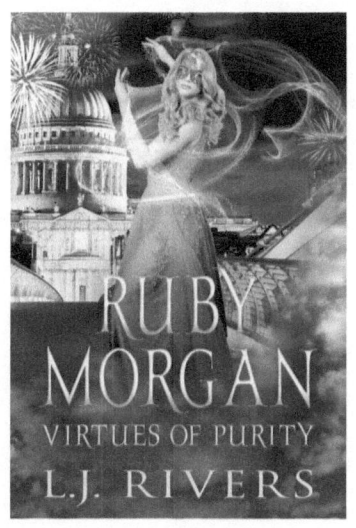